Shuttlecock

GRAHAM SWIFT was born in 1949 and is the author of many acclaimed novels, two collections of short stories (*England and Other Stories*, and *Learning to Swim and Other Stories*) and *Making an Elephant*, a book of essays, portraits, poetry and reflections on his life in writing. With *Waterland* he won the Guardian Fiction Prize (1983), and with *Last Orders* the Booker Prize (1996). Both novels have since been made into films. Graham Swift's work has appeared in over thirty languages.

Also by Graham Swift

The Sweet Shop Owner

Learning to Swim

Waterland

Out of this World

Ever After

Last Orders

The Light of Day

Tomorrow

Making an Elephant

Wish You Were Here

GRAHAM SWIFT

SHUTTLECOCK

PICADOR

First published 1981 by Allen Lane

First published by Picador 1997

This edition published 2010 by Picador
an imprint of Pan Macmillan, a division of Macmillan Publishers Limited
Pan Macmillan, 20 New Wharf Road, London N1 9RR
Basingstoke and Oxford
Associated companies throughout the world
www.panmacmillan.com

ISBN 978-0-330-51825-3

3 5 7 9 8 6 4

A CIP catalogue record for this book is available from
the British Library.

Visit www.picador.com to read more about all our books
and to buy them. You will also find features, author interviews and
news of any author events, and you can sign up for e-newsletters
so that you're always first to hear about our new releases.

SHUTTLECOCK

1

Today I remembered my hamster: my pet hamster, Sammy, a gift for my tenth birthday. It is over twenty years since my tenth birthday, since my hamster came to live in our house, but today I remembered it as if it still existed. I remembered its blond fur, its pink nose, its jet-black eyes which seemed, under certain circumstances, to be about to spill, like drops of ink, from its head. I remembered the sunflower seeds and bits of carrot we fed it and which, out of some primitive, needless instinct, it would cram into its pouches and unload about its cage in never-to-be-eaten piles. I remembered its noiseless feet, its stump of a tail; the way when I took it out of its cage for exercise it would never run across the room but always round the edges, following the skirting-board, in little furtive darts, between which it would freeze, one paw raised, head poised, in apprehension. And I remembered the day when my parents (who had already thrown Sammy's corpse into the kitchen boiler) said: 'We're sorry, there's something we've got to tell you . . .'

Why should I have thought of these things? They say you only recall what is pleasant and you only forget what you choose not to remember. Perhaps. But do I say 'remember'? This was not so much a memory as a pang . . .

You see, I used to torment my hamster. I was cruel to Sammy. It wasn't a case of wanting to play with him, or train him, or study how he behaved. I tortured him. Not at the very beginning. I loved the tiny thing that the man at the pet shop took from a warm heap of its fellows and installed in an aluminium cage for us. I wondered anxiously over the pale huddle of fur which for several days did nothing but whimper, cower and coyly excrete in its new home. But at some time after Sammy's arrival I made the discovery that this creature which I loved and pitied was also at my mercy.

When did the torturing begin? I used to turn my hamster on its back and pin it down with a finger across the belly while it made frantic wriggles to be free. I simulated a bird of prey, holding my hand two feet above it like a claw, while it crouched, mesmerized, in a corner. I cupped it inside my closed hands with scarcely space for air to enter, and then, slowly, made a gap between my thumb and finger – not enough for it to extricate itself, but enough for it to squeeze its head through in straining, strangulated efforts. Once, I opened our oven door . . .

And what was all this for? Will you believe me if I say it was all, still, out of love and pity? For love and pity hadn't disappeared. I needed only new means of eliciting them. Love ought to be simple, straightforward, but it isn't. All these cruelties were no more than a way of making remorse possible, of making my heart melt, of earning the doubtful luxury of putting my hamster away at the end of the day, a nervous jelly in its cage, and saying, my voice tight with contrition: 'I didn't mean it, Sammy. I didn't mean it. I love you, Sammy. Really.'

And today, twenty-two years later, coming home in the Tube, I went through it all again, saying to myself: I terrorized my hamster, I tormented a living thing. And I never . . .

But what made me think of these things?

It can have no connexion with the other outstanding event of the day: learning I am going to get Quinn's job. It all happened just before lunch. For the first time I can remember, Quinn was actually civil to me, even amiable. He called me up to his office on the pretext of looking over a report. He was his usual disagreeable, cantankerous self. And then, as he shut the report file, he came out with it. I'd never have thought it possible. It's what I've always wanted, of course – longed for – and even in some ways, I think, deserved. But I'd never have thought I had the slightest chance. I am the most senior amongst the assistant staff – but they don't always promote on seniority alone; they bring in people from outside. Quinn has a big say in the matter, and I've always thought that that old bastard had it in for me in no uncertain fashion. I would be the last person he'd want to see sitting in his seat. But this morning he closed the file and said quite casually: 'Oh, before you go, Prentis. This isn't definite, you understand – off the record and unofficial – but I think when I leave at the end of the summer you'll be taking over my place here.' He adjusted his glasses with a finger and thumb, and looked up at me through them. He has grey, mobile, darting eyes which his glasses sometimes hide and sometimes enlarge as if you're being looked at under a magnifying glass. 'You realize,' he said, 'for the time being, this is strictly between you and me.' Then he turned, with deliberate nonchalance, it seemed to me, to get on with his paperwork. I was so astounded I forgot to pick up the file I had brought in. As I reached the door he called me back. 'You'd better take this.' He tapped the file in a strange, slow way. 'We don't want things to get mislaid, do we?'

And he actually smiled.

I haven't told Marian yet. It's probably best, of course, to keep quiet about it until I hear something certain. There's no saying what games Quinn might be playing. But there's something else, something which I'm not sure I can explain, which stops me from telling Marian. Why shouldn't I tell my own wife, after all, about even a vague hint about my future prospects? It has something to do with the way I can never act simply and straightforwardly. Or about having thought about my hamster on the way home. When I got in today it was just an ordinary Monday evening and none of my family could have known that Daddy's promotion was on the cards. On Monday evenings I am particularly bad-tempered. My family knows it. I am bad-tempered most evenings, but Monday evenings are the worst. On Mondays I work late and don't get in till nearly eight. When I arrive, Marian comes out of the kitchen, wiping her hands on a tea-towel and brushing the hair from her eyes, and says, 'Hello, darling,' sheepishly, as if she has just woken up from some day-dream and she is surprised that I have come home at all. And the kids, who are glued to the television in the living-room, don't do anything.

Tonight they were watching *The Bionic Man* – or something like that, since there's a craze at the moment for films with heroes who are actually admired because they are half robots. I know it's probably my fault – because I'm the one who rents the television – but I don't like the way those two boys spend all their time stuck in front of it. It's not right; it's not the way children should grow up. I've been wanting for some time to get rid of that cursed little box. When we first got a television, years ago, we never thought of the boys, who were very young. It was more a present for ourselves, to relax with when we were tired – Marian after coping with the kids and I after work (I had just started, about then, in Quinn's section). But we soon discovered that neither of us really cared for TV. When I'm at home I like three things: reading and sleeping and, better than either of these, having sex; and Marian likes pottering around the house, tending her ferns and cactuses – that is, in between having sex – which I'm pretty sure she doesn't like any more, as I do. So, when the boys grew up, they started to usurp the television and establish special claims over it. And now it has become the focal point of their lives. Days have to be arranged according to the programmes they want to watch. Their sliding scale of bed-times, devised according to the best child-rearing manuals, has long since been abandoned to the demands of the air-waves. All this is bad enough; but when they can't take their eyes off the screen to say 'Hello' to their own father – that is too much.

I kissed Marian briskly and brushed past her. After all, she is at home when the kids come in from school –

she could stop this TV nonsense. I stood in the doorway to the living-room. 'Hello!' I said, and then again, more loudly, 'Hello!' Martin was sitting, both feet drawn up, cross-legged, in an armchair. In his lap was a plate with two or three digestive biscuits. He turned to look at me, actually biting, as he did so, on one of the biscuits. Peter lay, stomach down, on the floor, head propped in hands, feet in the air. He twitched his bottom.

I know they don't look up to me. That is the nub of the matter. My own sons don't look up to their father. They look up to the Bionic Man. The Bionic Man radiates Californian confidence. The Bionic Man performs imposs- ible feats, solves impossible riddles and bears no relation to anything natural. But they look up to him, not their father.

I give them three seconds. Then I cross the room, passing between them, switch off the television and in the same movement round upon them.

'Can't you give your Dad a hello when he comes in from work?'

Almost instantly they chime, in unison, 'Hello, Dad,' as if this will make me turn on the television again and go away.

I glower at them. I know I am going to go through my whole performance; after the angry indignation, the mock- ing lecture.

'What do you think this is?' I pat the top of the television. 'A machine, an object. It's full of wires and valves. And what do you think this is?' I touch my own breast. 'This is your Dad. Can you spot the difference?'

Peter, my younger son, aged eight, stifles a giggle and lowers his head.

'Right! Just for that, my boy – !'

I move suddenly forward to pull Peter up from the floor. I know I am about to act like an ogre, a madman – it's happened before (when did all this begin?) but I can't do anything about it. He tries to squirm free but I catch him by the collar. There is a moment when he swings obliquely, dangling in my grip, his sandalled feet not yet having found a footing on the floor, and just at this point, for some reason, I get a sudden mental vision of myself sitting in Quinn's leather chair. At the same time I glimpse Marian standing in the doorway. She has been watching my anger with a resigned, long-suffering expression – she's seen all this before too – but when I seize on Peter she bites her lip and clenches the tea-towel in her hand.

'Don't you smirk at your father when he's telling you off!'

Peter is on his feet now. I have my hands on his shoulders and I'm giving him a good, vigorous shaking. His little protuberant eyes bounce back and forwards on the end of his neck.

I finish with him, though he goes on shaking even when I've released him. Martin hasn't moved; he has a hand guiltily covering his biscuits.

'There'll be no more television for either of you! This evening or any evening! That's final. Do you hear? I said, do you—'

From both of them comes a thin, compliant 'Ye-es.'

And then, again, I know what is going to happen next. I can predict it like a scene in a play. Peter is going to cry. Not helpless tears, of shock and distress – though that is how they will seem, and they will be real enough tears – but tears that are quite perfectly timed and calculated. Both he and Martin know that I am easily beguiled by tears. I will even take back what I have said and say sorry, for tears. Underneath everything, they know that I am essentially a weak man. That's just the trouble. They know that when I rave at them and wallop them it's because I'm weak. That's why they don't say Hello and turn to look at me when I come in. So all this show of strength means nothing.

Sure enough, Peter starts to blubber.

'Huh!' I say. 'The Bionic Man never cries, does he?'

Peter's tears actually check slightly at this. But I have to think of something fast to avoid being swayed by them.

'Now, shall I tell you what you are going to do, right this very instant? You are going to go out into the garden – on this nice, warm evening – and you are going to – dig out all the weeds in the far flowerbed—' (even as I say this I remember that Marian has carried out precisely this task the previous afternoon) '—no, you are going to dig out all the stones, all the large stones, in *all* the flowerbeds, and put them in a *neat* pile by the compost heap. Do you understand? *Do you—*?'

'Ye-es.'

'And you say Hello to me when I come in – okay?'

'Ye-es.'

'Well out you go then!'

And later, if they had dared and wished to, the boys could have seen Marian and me, through the kitchen window, arguing like sparring fish in a tank. They would have seen me jerking my hands and pointing my finger and Marian clamping her hand over the top of her head, as though to hold it in place, the way she does when she argues. We nearly always argue after my outbursts with the kids. It's not so much that Marian takes issue with me for letting fly at them (she gave that up a long time ago) but that my tirades against the boys never seem to get used up or have sufficient effect with them alone and have to spill over onto Marian.

'We don't live at the top of a concrete block, do we? Or underground,' I add for some reason. 'We live in a house, with a garden. There's a common just up the road. Grass, trees. It's spring, isn't it?' I wave a hand towards the window. 'Warm weather. So why do they have to sit in front of the television all the time?'

'Yes! Yes! I'm not arguing with you! I'm not your children, am I? Ask them. Find out from them!'

'It's unnatural.'

'All right. Ask *them*. You're in charge.'

Through the window, Martin and Peter are crouched, backs half turned towards us, at the edge of one of the flowerbeds. It is already getting dark. They can probably hear Marian and me arguing. Our garden, like the gardens of the other houses in the road, is small – more a sort of extended back-yard. And it has a wall all the way round it so that anyone in it, viewed from the house, looks confined. Martin has a red polo-neck sweater and Peter a brown one and they both wear identical child's blue jeans. They seem to be going through some strange semblance of activity, half earnest, half ironic. There are no large stones in our well-dug flowerbeds. They are looking for these mysterious large stones.

'Tomorrow morning I want you to go down to that rental place and ask them to take our television back.'

'Oh come on!'

'I mean it. You do it. I thought you weren't arguing with me. I meant what I said tonight. You stop the payments and get them to take back the television.'

'I'm not going to do that.'

'Oh yes you are,' I say, grabbing Marian's arm and poking a finger almost into her face. 'Yes you bloody well are!' Her eyes bob just like Peter's.

And I'm suddenly astounded that all this is so predictable, and yet unpredictable too. Coming home and being bad-tempered and aggressive. As if every night I mean to be different. And tonight I had actually said to myself: a warm evening at the end of April; my interview with Quinn; my penitence on the train. I will say to Marian, 'Get an old crust of stale bread. Come with me. We're going to feed the ducks on Clapham Common.' You see, underneath, I am a soft-hearted man. I wouldn't even have minded if the kids had wanted to stay in watching television. So much the better. I've never told Marian about Quinn and what's going on at our office. There might have been ducklings on the pond, following their mothers – line astern. We'd have stood and thrown bread in the water. Marian would have been baffled. And perhaps I might have told her about my promotion.

But our life never has these tender moments. It's been like this for years.

2

I work in an office five minutes' walk from Charing Cross Underground, which is really a sub-department of the police. I hasten to add, I am not a policeman. I am more a sort of specialized clerk, an archivist. Our department has little to do with the day-to-day activities of the police – the police as the public think of them, the men in blue and conspicuous plain clothes. And yet it is an important, even an indispensable department.

Have you ever wondered what happens to the records of crimes that were committed long ago? Of police inquiries that took place up to a hundred years, or more, in the past? More to the point, have you ever wondered what happens to the records of crimes, or the evidence of possible crimes, relating to recent years, which because of some factor or other – often the death of the party or parties involved – have ceased to be acted upon? A suspected child-molester, for example, who commits suicide before proceedings can be taken, so that, after the inquest, the case is officially closed. Or an almost-successful embezzler who, being discovered after years milking the company funds, succumbs to a fortuitous coronary. All such records are the business of our department. In our vaults you will find the memorials of century-old murders, arsons, thefts and frauds – the delight of professional criminologists who, admitted only by the strictest permit, sit sometimes all day, at little lamp-lit reading desks, working through sheaves of yellowed documents. But you will find also – or you would find, if Quinn ever allowed you to – information relating to the living; information sometimes of a nefarious and inflammatory nature, the subjects of which would, to say the least, feel uneasy if they knew such information were stored, no matter how discreetly and inertly, in a police building. But it is not true – in case you are beginning to draw in your nostrils – that we keep files on people as such. Ours are distinct from ordinary police criminal records, where the criminal history of any person possessing one can quickly be referred to. We deal solely with individual cases, and ones which have been formally closed. In the official phrase, with 'dead crimes'.

What then is the object of our department? You will be surprised – the police are no fools. They know that every scrap of information is worth preserving. If in every hundred files only one contains a fact that may be useful in future, then it is worth keeping a hundred files. Before a case is closed, every avenue is checked first, so that what filters down to Quinn is only a tiny fraction of all that is handled. And once in our department, in the great majority of cases, there it stays, never to be touched again. But should some investigation yet-to-be discover a new link, should the material in our files prove relevant to some other case, it is instantly unearthed.

That is the main function of our department. But there is another. You may be surprised again: the police not only aren't fools, they consider their obligations too. What a relief from responsibility, what a weight off the official mind it would be if half the files in our office could be instantly destroyed. But they cannot be destroyed. And the police are aware of what possible harm might be done – not in the sense, of course, of direct incrimination, but in the damage done to reputations, livelihoods, personal trusts and confidences – if the contents of these files were revealed to the wrong people. We sit in a strong-room of secrets. We are custodians. Though custodians of what is often as much a mystery to us as to the public. For many of our files are sealed. Only Quinn can unseal and reseal them. And many are not only sealed but kept in safes and locked boxes which only Quinn can unlock.

What is it about institutions such as ours that invariably sites them underground? Most people, these days, go up from the street to work; we go down. We – that is, I and Quinn's other four assistants, Vic, Eric, Fletcher and O'Brien – work in a cavernous room half below and half above pavement level. Every morning we descend into this crypt. Around us rise shelves and cabinets stretching up to the ceiling, containing, for the most part, general indexes, inventories and cross-reference catalogues. The case files are kept in a series of rooms adjoining the inner wall of our offices, and then, going back chronologically as you descend, there are two more floors of archives below ours.

Quinn's own office occupies a privileged position on a superior level, like that of a bridge on a ship. The entrance to it is off a corridor on the ground floor of the building, but its rear wall forms the upper half of an end wall of our large room. He had some bizarre ideas, the architect responsible for converting our building. A back door and a small flight of stairs enable Quinn to communicate directly with our office; and a glass panel has been set in his rear wall, so if he wishes – and Quinn often does – he can look down at us as we work. Quinn has a large leather chair, a heavy, old-fashioned desk set on a maroon carpet, and an external window which looks out of one wing of our building (a solid, stony structure, by the way, of several decades' standing) where there is actually a strip of grass and three or four flowering cherry trees, one of them directly outside Quinn's window. The leather chair apart, Quinn's office is not luxurious – comfortable, imposing, but not luxurious. Doubtless, there are better appointed offices elsewhere in our building. But then I am not concerned, as it happens, with anyone beyond Quinn. And I envy Quinn his cherry tree and his daylight.

Although half our room is above ground level, there are no windows. The only natural light that filters in comes through one of those grilles of thick, opaque glass set into the pavement – which people walk over without noticing and which often denote underground public lavatories. In our case it is set into the ceiling at the far end from Quinn's office, where our room actually extends a little way, at basement level, under the pavement. You can stand beneath it and hear, surprisingly remote and faint, the clip-clop of people walking above. There is a general complaint that if only the glass were clear you could look up skirts. I ought to point out, incidentally, that in our immediate office there are no female staff.

And what do we do in this dungeon? Very few inquiries from outside are passed directly to the assistant staff. Our task, when this does happen, is routine: to consult the appropriate files, extract and collate the relevant information and draft a report to be sent, after vetting by Quinn, to the source of the inquiry. But only with the simplest and most straightforward queries are we allowed complete initiative. Most inquiries come via Quinn, so that, while we receive from him specific and express instructions, the reasons for them often remain obscure to us. And then a good many cases are handled solely by Quinn himself. Of these we know nothing.

What takes place with those cases that reach us is a sort of elaborate game of consequences – or, more accurately, hunt-the-thimble. Quinn has his own file index in his office. He gives one of us the code numbers of the files concerned and specifies the information to be extracted. Now, we are not necessarily told the purpose for which this information is to be obtained. In the case of complex inquiries where more than one file may be involved and several items of information have to be connected, we may work quite methodically and logically, but on quite false initial assumptions. Then Quinn shows us no mercy. He opens the back door of his office, waving the draft report of our findings. He stands at the top of his flight of stairs (Quinn scarcely ever comes down them; he has a slight limp in one leg, but I'm sure that's not what prevents him) and yells out the name of the culprit. 'Up here with you!' And you go. Since I am the senior assistant and am given the majority of these more involved inquiries, it is usually my name that is yelled, and I have to bear the humiliation of being singled out in front of my colleagues.

But this is not all. If, in the course of an inquiry, you need one of the sealed files or one of the files that are kept in Quinn's safe, you have to apply to Quinn himself for access to the contents. In such an event, Quinn will do one of three things. He will unseal or unlock the file and give it to you – no problem; or he will say, 'That's all right, I'll take over from here' – causing you no more trouble at least, but rendering all your previous work wasted; or – and this is worst – he will retain the sealed file in question, briskly say, 'I'll deal with this,' and tell you to carry out the remainder of the inquiry. Can you solve a mathematical problem if one of the factors needed to solve it is missing? And there is yet a further dilemma. Sometimes when looking up one of the files listed in Quinn's instruction, you discover it is missing – absent from the shelves. Now there is a ready explanation for this. It simply means that the file is one of those Quinn himself is using in one of the inquiries he handles alone. Obviously, you are obliged to point this out. You do. 'Excuse me, sir, but I think you must have this file – it's not on the shelf.' Quinn's reply on these occasions is never direct. 'Do I, Prentis? Do I? Hadn't you better check first that it hasn't been put in the wrong place?' He looks at you over the top of his glasses. And then, after an unpleasant pause and with a sigh that seems to condemn you for stupidity: 'All right, Prentis – I'll carry on from here.'

Do I begin to give the impression that something is *wrong* in our department?

When I first started in our office I must have accepted these anomalies, frustrating, baffling as they were, as part, nonetheless, of a 'system' – the way things had always been done and continued to be done, which it wasn't mine to question. Or perhaps it was true that when I first started things really were done in a more logical and sensible manner, which I have forgotten, and these peculiarities were a later development. I can't remember when I first began to find them unsettling. But I'm sure now, at any rate, that they are not part of any system. They are part of Quinn. They are part of that old bastard's obstinacy, mania, malice – whatever it is.

How can I best describe Quinn to you? I could say, in the manner of police descriptions, that he is shortish, about five-six; on the plump side; in his early sixties; balding; with spectacles and with a slight limp in his right leg. That he likes grey or dark blue suits; that his chubby face is often ruddy and cherubic (let's skip the police language); that his grey, soft hair is quite thick and glossy where it has not receded; and that his black-rimmed glasses are as much a means of hiding his eyes as of helping him to see. All this would be unexceptional. It might even suggest a podgy, harmless, quite benign little man. And that would be true. Quinn *does* look bumbly and benign. He has the sort of kindly, dimpled face which might be used in TV adverts to promote the 'home-made' qualities of some manufactured biscuit or pie. But it is precisely Quinn's apparent benignity and geniality which heighten his real coldness, his severity, his ruthlessness. Could I be wrong? Could I have mistaken and perverted some quite innocuous truth? Could I have exaggerated my boss's vindictiveness because I have set my sights (I don't deny it) on one day having his job? That is a common enough story. But I don't think so. When a man sets you difficult or impossible tasks and then summarily blames you when you fail to complete them – that is vindictiveness.

And it's not as if I haven't tried the sympathetic view. Could Quinn be ill in some way? Could he be suffering some kind of breakdown? (I have had some experience of breakdowns – but I will come to that later.) Could he be going off the rails from overwork? The answer to that question is: yes – and no. Quinn does work extremely hard. He often stays in his office late into the night – his light shining purposefully through the glass panel when you yourself are winding up a late day. But I get the distinct impression that this extra work Quinn does is more by choice and design than obligation. And when you enter his office on some fleeting and innocent errand – merely to bring him a routine document he has asked for – the picture you get, as you wait for him to raise his head, is of a man happily – I repeat, happily – and earnestly engaged in his tasks. A man pleased with his efforts and sure of their usefulness. It is only when he looks up and says, with a scowl, 'What is it?' – as if you have encroached on his contentment – that any discord enters the scene. And then it seems that you are to blame for it.

So, if that picture – of Quinn contentedly beavering away in his leather chair while outside the cherry tree waves at his window – does not capture his true malice, what does? I will tell you. It is when, at moments during the day, he gets up from his desk and – sometimes for minutes on end – looks down at us through his glass partition. If you look up then, as you only dare do for a brief, disguised instant, you see him framed in the rectangular panel. He stares at us with the air of a scientist surveying some delicate experiment. His face is stern and gloating. He rests his hands against the glass, and the tips of his fingers and the balls of his thumbs go white. It is then that I know that Quinn is evil – I hate him. It is then that I know too, most clearly, that I envy him.

And let me tell you just two or three things that have

been puzzling me – and still are – despite Quinn's almost incredible remarks yesterday about my promotion. Firstly, those lists of file-items which Quinn gives me to investigate – they are getting remarkably long. It is rare for any one case to involve more than two or three files, but Quinn sometimes has me scouring through five or six – and in some instances I cannot find *any* relation between the material in one file and the next. Secondly, those missing files which I assume Quinn is working on himself (it would explain those late nights of his) do not reappear. I have watched. Even after weeks they are not back in their places. Thirdly, none of the other assistants says anything – only the usual quiet passing complaints about 'bloody Quinn'. I am beginning to think that it's only me Quinn is playing games with.

But I didn't mean to talk about Quinn, or about my problems. I meant simply to tell you about my work. I'm not the only one who has a tiresome job or a difficult boss. And I don't want to give the impression that because we work in a dungeon, we are prisoners. That we don't emerge at lunch-time, like everyone else, and make for the pub on the corner (Quinn, by the way, works through lunch); that we can't go through, more or less when we like, to our ancillary offices and typing pool, beyond the file rooms, and joke with the girls (there is a new one at the moment called Maureen with extremely thrusting breasts). There is nothing exceptional about our job.

But I hear you say, Yes, there is, and in an interesting, an exciting way. Something to do, you're thinking, with the thrill of detective work. I used to think that too once, when I first began. I used to think of all those stories which no one ever knows about, all those buried secrets, hidden away in our files. It must have shown, because Quinn once said to me (here I go again about Quinn): 'You've got a rich imagination, haven't you, Prentis? A lurid imagination. That doesn't help, you know, in this job.' It was the first personal remark I can remember him making, and he said it with a frosty look and a scowl, and I resented it. But it was true. You soon learn to forgo the thrill of detection in our department. To begin with, we are not detectives – that is somebody else's job. We are only, as it were, specialized librarians. What blander job is there than a librarian's? And then, as with any work, ours too is routine. Most of the time is spent in mundane chores like cataloguing and indexing. Real inquiries don't come our way thick and fast (though they've been getting ever more frequent recently). And even here the law of routine applies. No matter how extraordinary the material you work with, it becomes, when it's your daily business to deal with it – unextraordinary.

But then again, I'm wrong. It isn't like that. I'm trying to say something, perhaps, that I don't really feel at all. It's in the nature of routine not so much to make things ordinary as to numb you against recognizing how remarkable they are. And you'd be surprised at some of the things contained in our files. You'd be appalled at the black and desperate picture of the world they sometimes offer. In certain corners of our office there are some gruesome little collections – which we have to consult quite often – which consist of police pathologists' findings and coroners' reports on cases in which there has been police interest. I have dipped into these files too many times to think much about them; and yet sometimes I am suddenly startled –

the bubble of routine bursts around me – when I actually stop to contemplate some of the things that pass through my hands.

Here, for example, is a piece of 'routine' that I dealt with only last week. The police, of course, closed the case. The whole thing was handed over to psychiatrists – and it's a psychiatrist (psychiatrists are some of our most frequent customers) who wants to dig it out again now. It seems that a woman, who has since died, had to nurse her husband, at home, during an illness that eventually proved fatal. The husband had been – I shan't mention names – a figure of some renown in his field. During the later stages of the illness the wife refused to have the husband admitted to hospital and, after a certain time, to allow any medical supervision whatsoever. As well as the husband and wife, there was a son, aged eleven. When the husband died, the wife not only failed to inform the authorities or to do anything with the corpse but adamantly believed that her husband was not, in fact, dead. Furthermore, she turned viciously against the son, accusing him of being responsible for what had happened to the father. Some days after the death, the wife locked the boy up with the corpse and told him he would not be let out until he had brought his father back to life again. What the boy *thought*, shut up like this with his dead father, is conjecture. What he *did* was clear enough when the matter came to light two days later. He found a penknife, belonging to the dead man, in one of the bedroom drawers, and with it – for reasons never established, though according to the boy himself, 'to find out what his father was made of – systematically disfigured and mutilated his father's body.

And all this you have to bring home to a wife who tends house-plants and two healthy kids whom you take out on the common at weekends to play with frisbees and cricket bats.

3

I travel home on the Tube. The Northern Line: seven stops to Clapham South. Up, out of the ground, and then down into it again. I am struck by the way people behave on the Tube. They look at each other beadily and inquisitively, and something goes on in their thoughts which must be equivalent to the way dogs and other animals, when they meet, sniff each other's arses and nuzzle each other's fur. But animals do this innocently and – who knows? – with affection. What goes on in the Tube is done with suspicion and menace. It is as if everybody is trying to search out everybody else's story, everybody else's secret, and the assumption is that this secret will always be a weakness; it must be something unpleasant and shameful which will make it possible for its owner to be humiliated and degraded. The fact that I am making these observations makes it clear, of course, that I am guilty myself of the activity I am describing. But look at any group of people in an Underground train. You won't see much laughter, smiling, or even talk. Not nearly as much, at least, as you'll see in any bus or railway carriage travelling through the genial daylight. Ignore the people whose faces are conveniently sunk in books and magazines. Watch the eyes of the others. Am I right? Everyone is trying to strip everyone else bare, and everyone, at the same time, is trying not to be stripped bare himself. Oh yes, I know, in one sense, this is almost literally true. Half the men in the carriage are mentally removing the clothes of the girls who are strap-hanging near the doors. They are titillated by their stretched arms, by the little ovals of sweat which appear at the armpits on their blouses. But, beyond this, something deeper, something darker, is going on. Am I right?

Now and then, when I travel on the Tube, I get this feeling that something terrible and inevitable is going to happen. All those bodies crammed together, all those furtive faces searching each other. All this mystification. And I can't help thinking of the populations of animals which live in burrows – rats, lemmings – which (I read somewhere) exist in far greater concentrations than any human population. When I get out at Clapham South, up into the air, past the newsstand and the florist's, I breathe a deep breath of relief. Opposite the station is the common – criss-crossed and encircled by incessant chains of ill-tempered traffic – but it is the common. It's spring. There are daffodils nodding near the bowling-green on my walk home; the sticky-buds are opening on the chestnuts, and there are catkins on the silver birches. There is no doubt what commons are for. They are proof that, huddled as we are in cities, we couldn't live without trees and grass, at the expense of no matter what urban convenience. And this need crops up in many ways. Marian, for example, as I've already mentioned, keeps indoor plants. In the winter, when the garden is dead and colourless, our house still sprouts with leaves. And whenever I am in one of my moods, Marian talks to her plants. It's true. Going round with her plastic watering-can, she has whole conversations with them.

Have I described my wife? She is thirty-two. She has sandy-blond hair, straight and light so that when the wind catches it, it blows, in a rather clichéd but, for all that, artless way across her face. She has a slender, supple and still provocative figure, even though she has been a mother for ten years. I am particularly grateful that she hasn't slumped as some women do after they have had their children. You could say that my wife has her share of beauty. Why does that statement half catch me unawares? Her face is a little on the long side, but because her mouth is full and her eyes large (blue, with little chips of green in them), you wouldn't notice this. She has a way of lowering her eyes and then raising them and suddenly opening them wide when someone speaks or when something claims her attention, as if she spends all her life far away, in a trance – which is not to say that she cannot be alert, even athletic. This blank, startled expression sometimes makes me feel (it is a strange thing to say, I admit) that she doesn't know who I am. Before we were married and we had Martin and Peter she worked as a physiotherapist in a hospital. She likes pale colours, but I prefer her in dark ones. Her complexion is smooth, on the pale side, and is one of those complexions which never change very much with mood or emotion – which suggest passivity or concealment. But the thing I like most about Marian (excuse me again if this sounds odd) is her malleability, her pliancy; the feeling I get that I could mould and remodel her (she must have learnt a thing or two at that physiotherapy clinic), contort and distort her, parcel her up and stretch her into all kinds of shapes, but, just as you can work a piece of clay a thousand times but still have left the same piece of clay, she would still, at the end of it all, be Marian. Marian.

4

When Quinn called me in yesterday I should have taken my opportunity to confront him about the missing files. When he said, 'We don't want things to get mislaid, do we?' and gave that knowing smile, that was surely a hint. I should have taken my cue and said, 'Talking of mislaid files . . .' What a cowardly man I am.

But let me tell you what passed between us before Quinn mentioned my promotion. We were discussing the report I had brought in, which merely required his approval before being sent off. I won't bore you with details. When we discuss such things we talk in a sort of code (people, when you think about it, spend a lot of their time talking in code). Quinn sat in his black leather, brass-studded chair, I stood at his shoulder. A band of sunlight spread from the window, and I was tempted to say, 'The cherry tree is looking nice, sir' – the sort of chirpy, fatuous remark that is really unthinkable in our office. Quinn's hair smelt very slightly of some sort of lotion. On the wall, behind his desk, above a black filing cabinet, is a photograph showing several lined-up army officers – one of which I assume to be Quinn, though I have never had the chance to look that closely – and dated April '44. It's about the only personal item in Quinn's entire office. Quinn approved of my report and pushed it briskly to one side. He sniffed vigorously and pinched the bridge of his nose. 'Now what about C9? How are you getting on with that?' (C9 is the reference number of a case I am currently working on; it's not the real number, of course – I couldn't tell you that.)

Now C9 happened to be one of those cases for which Quinn himself had given me instructions but in which certain of the file items proved to have virtually no connexion at all. For example, File B in the series contained information relating to X (now deceased), a former civil servant, sacked for alcoholic incompetence and later arrested for a number of petty frauds and sexual offences, who had made allegations against a certain Home Office official, Y – allegations subsequently investigated (without Y's knowledge, either of the allegations or the investigation) and found to be false. X died of a heart attack while undergoing trial. File C in the series contained no reference to X or Y, but was a report on another Home Office official, Z, apparently unconnected, professionally or personally, with Y (or X), who had committed suicide (by stepping in front of an Underground train) shortly after the secret investigations on Y. This death was subsequently thoroughly investigated, with negative results as far as officialdom was concerned – but with great distress to the unfortunate widow, who had to reveal, under pressure, intimate details about her and her husband's personal life: the mess of their marriage, his sexual incompetence, his cruelty to her, his attempting once to sleep with his nineteen-year-old daughter, an assault on his son with a garden knife, etc,

etc. File D in the series was even remoter from X and Y, and File E was not on the shelves. As for the reasons for the C9 inquiry – some new evidence which had come retrospectively to light – Quinn was hanging on to this himself.

When Quinn asked me about C9 I think I looked at him for signs of madness.

'I'm sorry, sir. I'm having some difficulty in connecting some of the items. If I could—'

I knew what was coming. When you are in Quinn's office you are the luckless schoolboy hauled before the headmaster.

'Good God, Prentis! How long have you had C9 – and how long have you been in this department? You realize I entrust you with these more important cases because you're the senior assistant. You realize that, don't you?'

'Yes.'

'Good. And you've made no headway?'

I know what he wanted me to say. He wanted me to say that there was a connexion between X and Z. The obvious thing. But if I said this I knew what his retort would be: 'So there's a connexion between X and Z. Proof? Lurid imagination, Prentis, lurid imagination. No good in this job.'

'Perhaps – if I had a little more information to work on?'

(File E, for instance.)

Quinn cupped his hands, behind his head and made his leather chair swivel slightly from side to side. He seemed to be waiting for something. He is one of those men who maintains his authority even though he may be sitting, in a nonchalant posture, and you are standing, close by him, looking down at him. He looked at me steadily, the light from the window reflected in his glasses. Some of the grey hairs round the fringes of his scalp are really a pure white. The scalp itself gleams like pink wax. And then, as often happens when I'm face to face with Quinn, I found myself hurriedly, and for no apparent reason, revising my impression of him. No, not mad – whatever Quinn is, he isn't mad. And I had this sudden urge to say to him, in all sincerity: I don't understand. Please tell me. You see, I don't understand at all.

'More information? Good heavens, limited information is why we're here, Prentis. If we had all the information we wanted, we'd be gods, wouldn't we?'

We know very little about Quinn personally in our office. It's generally believed he's a divorcee or an old bachelor. For some reason, as he looked at me I felt quite sure he could not be a father.

'Very well. I'll take over C9. If you'll bring me all you have . . .' He took his hands from behind his head and gave a resigned snort. 'And you'd better make your final draft of this.' He took the folder containing the original report we had been discussing, closed it and pushed it towards me across the desk.

'Oh – before you go –'

And then it was that he became, in a single instant, amiable, confiding – and up came the subject of my promotion.

So unexpected was this turn of events that my first response was disbelief. Why should he have chosen this moment to raise my hopes, after having humbled me and effectively slandered my competence? Why should he have thrown me off balance if not for some hidden, ulterior motive? As he spoke of 'off the record' and 'strictly between you and me' I had an odd idea. Supposing he clearly read my suspicions about the office 'system'? Supposing I was being tested? Could my promotion to Quinn's position be conditional upon my speaking up, like a responsible and dutiful under-officer, and voicing my suspicions? Or could it be that this mention of promotion had no real basis at all (I am still wondering this), that it was just another of his little games to confuse and harass me?

When he tapped the file I had my chance. I could have said: 'Sir, there's something I feel I should . . .' or: 'Sir, I can't help having noticed . . .' But I didn't. How was I to know that I wasn't jumping to conclusions? And how was I to know that speaking up might not actually jeopardize my perfectly genuine promotion, and it was precisely for keeping quiet that it was being offered to me? Quinn was doubtless enjoying my dilemma.

'I'm something of an old work-horse, Prentis,' he said in a candid tone quite unlike him. 'I've been sitting here for too long, stopping young blood from taking my place.'

He smiled. Dimples appeared in his cheeks.

I suppose what stopped me saying anything in the end was not my rather hasty speculations but simply the old, accustomed fact of Quinn's authority. The headmaster and the schoolboy again. You may have your suspicions, your fears, you may even believe there is something, somewhere, terribly, drastically wrong, but because someone else is in charge, because there is a part of the system above you which you don't know, you don't question it, you even distrust your own doubts. It's like the people in the Tube. They may be seething to rise up, to protest, to commit unspeakable acts against normality, but because someone has seen to it that there are Underground trains for them to be on and because some system makes sure that they keep shuttling and circling through the dark, and that is how it will be, today, tomorrow and the day after that – they don't.

Quinn turned his face for a moment towards the window. He looked at the cherry tree. Then he turned back to me.

'Something you want to say, Prentis?'

The old bastard.

'No.'

What a weak, what a cowardly man I am.

5

And why did I want a pet hamster?

It was because of the hamster we kept in our classroom at primary school – in a green cage, beside the dank-smelling sink where we used to wash out paint brushes and jam jars. Every week two of us would be chosen as monitors to look after the hamster, to feed it and clean out its cage, and every Friday one lucky person would be selected to take the hamster home, to be its guardian over the weekend.

Our class-master was a man called Forster. Perhaps it was Forester, but that, maybe, is just fanciful association. One of the subjects Mr Forster used to teach us was Nature Study. From what I gather from Martin and Peter, Nature Study is not a subject they teach any more in primary schools – and that, I can't help thinking, is a bad thing. Our school was in Wimbledon. There is quite a lot of Nature in Wimbledon, as London suburbs go; but I never really thought of Nature as something ordinary and familiar. Mr Forster's twice-weekly lessons gave me an impression of Nature as a rare and mysterious commodity. I didn't think of it as a principle, as a word, or even as a collection of multifarious items, like the pictures of buds and toadstools Mr Forster drew on the blackboard. I saw it as a stuff, which could be gathered, or mined like gold, if only you knew where to find it. Above all, it was something quite separate and distinct from me.

Our class-room was a dim, gloomy room with a view of a dim, walled-round asphalt playground. I don't remember it too well, but I remember its smell: a mixture of chalk, floor-polish, water-colour paints and the various, spicy and ever-fascinating smells of my class-mates. In those days I registered other people not by their names and all the other identity tags but by smells and indefinable peculiarities. As if people were really only, somehow, indistinct outlets from which exuded scents, hints of some far-off source. I have forgotten the names of my class-mates, but I still remember their smells. There were certain girls who had a sharp ammoniac smell, and certain boys with a soft, dull smell, like that of much-used India rubber. Mr Forster had a reassuring, reliable smell, like the smell of wood, and just above his upper lip he had a strange and intriguing birth-mark, like some dark, fossilized fruit. As for myself, I believed I was odourless and nondescript – as if I were made from something that didn't exist.

Then one day Mr Forster carried into the class-room this green cage with a wire-mesh front and something living inside it. And in producing the hamster before us, like a conjuror, he used the words – as if he were revealing to us a fragment of some precious lost treasure – 'a part of nature'. It was these words, I swear it, and not any sentimental child's craving for a 'pet', for a fluffy thing with legs, which sowed the seeds of my desire for a hamster of my own. How conscientiously I carried out my duties, when it came to my turn, as weekly monitor. How yearningly I waited for my moment, which was only to come once in the school year, to bear the hamster home on Friday afternoon. How jealously I longed to possess a part of nature.

But, when my parents at last yielded and took me one Saturday to the pet shop, what became of this reverence? Did I get up every morning to take out my little golden piece of nature, cherish, love and adore it? No. I turned into this sadist, this power-monger, this refiner of cruelties. What became of my love? For what else is love – don't tell me it is anything less simple, less obvious – than being close to nature? What became even of my possessiveness? I remember that near the back door of our house in Wimbledon there was a little kitchen garden, a patch of walled-in earth in which my mother planted mint, sage, parsley and, for good measure, a clump of lavender (these plants, by the way, she used to talk to, just like Marian). On this patch of earth, one warm day, I once made the experiment of letting out my hamster from its cage. When it was placed on the ground it sniffed cautiously at first. Then instinct took hold of it. Making a sudden dash for the corner of the patch, it began tunnelling, at a staggering speed, into the earth. I made a move to pull it back by the hind legs. But I had been so taken by surprise, and it was digging so frantically that by the time I attempted this it was already too deep to be grasped. I could see its pink tail-stump and frenetic haunches disappearing beyond recovery. I recall quite distinctly what my feeling was at this moment. It was not fear that I might lose my precious hamster, as indeed might have happened. It was outrage, it was fury, that it had got itself into a position where I no longer had control over it. I started to claw blindly at the soil. In fact, I need not have worried. Instinct had returned, but without a clear sense of direction. The little thing had tunnelled into one of the corners of the patch, and after a short while it came up against the concrete foundations of the retaining walls. Here it huddled, enjoying a few moments of spurious liberty, before my digging hands discovered it. Needless to say, I punished it severely.

Now let me tell you something. We are all looking for a space where we can be free, where we cannot be reached, where we are masters. Let me tell you something else – about my hamster. Before I got it I was a pretty unruly child – the only child of my parents but more, very often, than they could cope with. I made their life hell at times – my father's wallopings and my mother's exasperated pleas proved it. Once I even bit my father's hand and I swear my teeth touched the raw bone in his finger. At school Mr Forster – or Forester – was about the only teacher who could command my obedience. But after I had my hamster all this changed. I became a docile, dutiful, even an exemplary son. The 'Conduct' entries on my school reports underwent complete transformation. I remember it was that year that I actually volunteered to read the lesson in morning assembly – 'Consider the lilies' if I recall it correctly – and that I astonished my parents by little kindnesses such as making tea for them on Sunday mornings and offering to weed the garden. And all that changed again when my hamster – my golden hamster, my Sammy whom I remembered today with such pangs – died.

6

When we went to bed Marian raised again the issue of the television. It is not that she is argumentative (haven't I already pointed out that my wife's principal attraction is her pliancy?) or that she would care herself if we dispensed with the television. But she acts as a kind of automatic counter-weight to my relations with my sons. Sometimes I think she is scarcely aware of doing it. If she thinks I have been too hard on them, she doesn't stop me at once, but she tries, later, to put some separate, compensatory restraint on me. She doesn't take my sons' side against me. She knows better than that. But something in her, almost independent of her, wants stubbornly to restore the balance, like water finding its level – and it's not easy to ignore. Perhaps this is her subtle and discreet way out of a difficult and hazardous predicament – for if I ever found her deliberately siding with my sons, I know – and she knows – what I would do. I would hit her. But it isn't like that. This something in her is almost involuntary, it is almost part of her pliancy.

After our set-to over the television, for example, I did not let the boys come in from their punishment in the garden till after night-fall. Not only did they have to search for non-existent stones but they had to do so in the dark as well. When Marian tried to go out to fetch them in I held her by the arm. It was not until nearly nine – a good half-hour after dusk – that I went out myself to have the satisfaction of seeing their bewildered, chastened faces as they trooped in.

And now, a few hours later, in bed, because of this (in her view) excessiveness on my part, Marian was once more questioning my threat to have our television removed – not with the bluster of our earlier row in the kitchen, but with the neat, just and almost disinterestedly expressed argument that since I had already made my point by my stern penalty, wouldn't it be going too far to confiscate the television as well?

All the time Marian was pleading in this way I was making adjustments to her body and manoeuvring her limbs into one of my favourite positions for love-making. I won't go into exact details; it is something developed over the years which requires a little setting up. Marian is quite accustomed, almost indifferent to these preparations. She lies back, lets me continue and lets herself go like putty. I was determined, you see, to take my consolation for a taxing day.

She kept on talking. 'So I'm not taking that television back,' she concluded, firmly – though hardly in a posture that went with command. It was rather as if she were saying (it's a kind of argument which Marian is always, in a way, silently, wearily advancing): 'See what I'm letting you do to me, I don't resist one bit, I let you go ahead – and you still want everything your own way.'

'All right, all right,' I said. I had almost finished my

adjustments, had become quite aroused in the process, and now the matter of the television seemed not so important after all. I was ready to take my place in the structure of flesh I had been building.

'Now—' I said.

And then Marian said: 'Tough' – in a quite mild voice. 'I haven't put my doo-dah in.'

When Marian says her 'doo-dah' she means her diaphragm. I looked her in the face – which was not, in fact, in our present position, such an easy action. I knew she was probably lying. But I didn't risk it. Martin and Peter are enough by themselves.

I held out for a few more, tormented seconds. I thought to myself: now is the time when I could tell her about my promotion. This might break the impasse. Then she might say: 'Oh – it's all right darling – I've got my doo-dah in really' – and give some coaxing wiggle.

But I didn't. I said: 'I'll bloody well take the television back myself.'

7

Today –

But you will have gathered by now that I am writing all this as thoughts come to me and as things happen. I have broken off since I last wrote, time has passed, and when I say 'today' I mean, of course, today, a day later – Wednesday to be precise. I don't know that I ever intended to put pen to paper again, or, indeed, to write as much as I have already. It all began when I remembered my hamster in the Tube and I had this urge to set down my feelings and try to account for them. It's strange, I've never really wanted to put them on paper before. And then it seemed, no sooner had I written that first confession than there were lots of other things that had to be examined and written down – and now I'm at it again. I don't know where it's getting me. It's not as if anything extraordinary is happening. But I feel I have to go on.

Today I went to visit Dad. I go to see Dad most Wednesday evenings, and often on Sundays too. Dad lives in a mental hospital. It's fair to use the word 'lives' because he has been there now for nearly two years. He is not insane, you understand. Most people who live in mental hospitals are not insane; they just have, like people in ordinary hospitals, some particular thing or other wrong with them. If you saw Dad now you would see nothing alarming. Quite the opposite. He is an upright, robust, distinguished-looking man in his late fifties. He has always had a good physique, a strong, intelligent, photogenic face – like the face of some seasoned explorer or mountaineer – and all these imposing features, this statuesque quality, are now, if anything, accentuated. But nearly two years ago he had some sort of sudden breakdown, as a result of which he went into, for want of a better word, a kind of language-coma. I haven't heard Dad speak since. For two years I have been visiting this silent shell. That is all that is odd about him. Now the doctors say that there is no physical reason that they, at least, can discover why Dad shouldn't speak. In that sense his condition is 'psychological'. But what they don't know for certain is whether Dad can understand anything of what is spoken to him or if he can even recognize people around him. In order to know that, Dad would have to be able to tell them. Oh, I speak to Dad myself, of course. I have long, rambling conversations with him – like Marian with her plants – in which I even reply to things which I suppose Dad might have said. But all I ever see in his eyes is a filmy gaze, fixed on the distance, which now and then settles on me as on some curious object. And all that ever emerges from his lips are inarticulate sounds – coughs, grunts, clearings of the throat.

Nobody knows the cause of Dad's breakdown – or, if it comes to it, whether what was involved was a true mental breakdown or some sort of seizure of the brain. At the time, there was nothing in my Dad's circumstances which would have seemed capable of triggering off such a crisis. A year before his own trouble, it's true, my mother died quite suddenly and apparently in perfect health (she simply collapsed one day on the kitchen floor – it's a day, to be honest, I don't like to remember in detail), and if any event might have led to my father's breakdown, this was it. I have never doubted – since I began to consider such things (and that, of course, was after my pre-hamster days of tantrums and rebellion) – my father's feeling for my mother. I have always thought that his command, his confidence and poise, owed much to her, and that she in turn derived her calm, her contentment from his success. Since I got married myself I have looked up, almost in awe, to the solidarity of their partnership, their health, stability, their ease. If any event . . . But my father did not crumble at my mother's death. He bore it, yes, with grief, but with a noble (and it was only then that I began to think of that word as appropriate to my father) resignation. All this admiration, I should add, I have never shown, not to my father's face – quite the opposite. He was a partner in a successful firm of consultant engineers. He had an office with a thick, plush carpet and enormous chairs. After my mother's death he worked on as energetically as ever, no doubt with a certain inner hollowness, but (for reasons I will come to) he was a popular, a respected man, he had plenty of friends and business connexions with which to fill his time. Then one day, a year later, he cracked up completely. Nobody can say why. And nobody can say if my Dad will ever recover.

When I go to visit him we always follow the same ritual. Dad lives in a ward with about twelve other patients, all in their fifties and sixties. For the most part, gentle, amiable-looking men in dull dressing-gowns with piping round the cuffs and tasselled cords. Now that the weather is warm, and as the ward is on the ground floor, they are usually sitting outside when I arrive, grouped in wicker chairs on the little terrace outside the tall ward windows, smoking, talking, reading the papers or playing board games. Dad sits amongst them, but not taking part in any of their activities. When I appear I say hello to them all, and a broken chorus answers me. Then I say hello to Dad in particular. His eyes flicker. He recognizes me. But I don't know if he recognizes me as his son or only as the person who comes to see him on Wednesdays and Sundays. He gets up – sometimes he does this automatically and sometimes I have to put a hand on his arm – and we go for a slow stroll round the hospital grounds. We sit for a while on one of the wooden benches placed here and there on the lawns and 'chat'. Then we stroll back to the group outside the ward windows and I have conversations with some of the others in which I somehow pretend Dad is taking part. In the winter, of course, we cannot take our stroll outside. Then we walk up and down the corridors (the hospital is run on liberal lines and is quite tolerant about this), and we visit the canteen where the more capable patients can come and go as they please. But I don't like these indoor meetings so much. In the corridor we have to pass other patients, some of whom jibber, jerk their heads and even yell out loud (though I have learnt after two years' visits that such things are nothing to be alarmed at). But passing by these patients makes me think that my Dad is only another indiscriminate member of the ranks of the mad.

Of course, there is something terribly perfunctory, terribly pointless and mechanical about these twice-weekly visits. Sometimes I think it is not a man who walks or sits beside me, but some effigy I push and trundle about on a wheeled trolley, and it is I who am the deranged one for imagining this dummy is really alive, is my own father. When we sit on our bench (we have our favourite one, beneath a cedar tree) there is this feeling of hopeless pantomime. But then, on the other hand, there is so much to be *said*, so much to be explained, understood and resolved between us. It is odd, but until Dad ceased to speak I never had this need to talk to him. And because Dad does not answer back, because he neither hinders nor encourages whatever I say, I use him as a sort of confessional. I go to Father to say things I would never say anywhere else. (Perhaps I *am* the deranged one, after all.)

Tonight, for example, I said: 'The boys have been bad again this week. Trouble-making, insolent. What's wrong with them, Dad? I've been down on them again, and I've been bullying Marian and I've threatened to take back our television. And I don't mean any of it, not really, though I'm going to go through with it . . .' Dad looks in front of him, as if he is looking at some phenomenon in the middle distance which only he has noticed. His eyebrows are thick; pale brown hairs mixed with grey. The little furrows above his straight nose, the firm set of his lips suggest some inscrutable resolution. His hands rest on his knees, and now and then they move automatically, rubbing the cloth of his trousers. Between the knuckles on the first finger of his right hand is the little bluish scar where I bit him when I was a boy. 'What do you say?' I ask. 'Nothing, eh?' For, even after two years, I still treat Dad's silence as if it is some quirky thing of the moment and not a permanent fact. And even after two years, because I can't help feeling that Dad's silence is some punishment, some judgement against me, I sometimes say to him, in all ingenuousness: 'Please Dad, please. Speak to me. Explain.'

It's peaceful in the hospital grounds these spring evenings, as the light fades and the more disturbed patients are ushered inside and put to bed. In some ways I would rather be there, sitting with Dad under the cedar tree, than in my own back garden at home, or even with Marian feeding the ducks on the common. The hospital is like an old red-brick country house of another age, set amidst trees. Except for the blue and white notices, the modern extensions and the iron bars across the lower windows, you wouldn't know. There are rose beds, yew walks, ornamental ponds and the sort of sculptural trees (cedars, maples, copper beeches) that you associate with private estates. All this is surrounded by a high brick wall; and the hospital grounds themselves are set within fields and woodland, though the suburbs of South London are less than a mile away. It's a strange thing that we put mad people in these walled-in parks, as if we recognize that though they have to be confined they need to rub against nature. But then, as I've said, the people in mental hospitals aren't mad, no – or if they behave like mad people, this is only what you'd expect in such a place – so there seems nothing abnormal about it.

Since I've been visiting Dad I've been making my own private study of the inmates. I cannot decide, still, whether they are prisoners or whether in some way, unlike you or me, they have broken free. Don't we all, secretly, want to have their privileges? The hospital staff cheerfully condone behaviour that elsewhere would, to say the least, be frowned upon; and the same indulgence is somehow expected from visitors. It's like entering a foreign country where you must bide by the native customs. So when you see a man walking down a corridor with what looks like – and, indeed, it is – a turd in his hand – you say nothing. Or when a figure, in an apparently drugged lethargy, at one end of the ward, suddenly starts to beat his head, in archetypal fashion, against the metal bars of a bed-frame, you do not stop and stare.

Only once have I seen the hospital staff perturbed on behalf of their visitors' sensibilities. This was almost a year ago, a Sunday afternoon, when the weather was especially hot. The inmates were scattered over the lawns, some lying in little groups, some sitting with visiting relatives, some sprawled alone, in shady places, fast asleep. Some of them wore handkerchiefs with the corners tied in knots over their heads as sun-hats, and this fashion seemed to have caught on, like the crazes which sometimes sweep through children's playgrounds, so that the only activity seemed to be the appropriating of handkerchiefs, the making and trying-on of the finished caps. The nursing staff, with their white jackets, were also lounging drowsily on the grass, and nobody seemed to mind their apparent non-vigilance. I was sitting with Dad, not on our usual bench under the cedar – somebody had got there first – but on one of the five or six benches ranged in front of the rose beds. This is a popular place for visitors, and on fine Sunday afternoons each rose-bowered bench is occupied by a patient and usually a middle-aged or elderly couple. Some of these visitors are often quite smartly dressed – like the sedate old couples I see sometimes watching the bowls matches on Clapham Common – the women in pastel suits, hats and white gloves, the men in linen jackets. And I swear they come on these visits because they actually enjoy it – a day out to some exclusive private garden.

In the midst of this general relaxation I suddenly noticed – several other eyes must have noticed it too, but the odd thing was that this event went, at first, quite unregistered – that one of the patients on the edge of a group away to our right was removing his clothes. He was a tall, gaunt man – over seventy, I would have said – with white hair, in a grey hospital suit. Before anyone made a move to stop him he had taken off not only his suit but his underwear as well. An attendant stood up, shouted at him, and immediately the patient broke into a loping run, not, it seemed, to escape pursuit, for his run had nothing urgent about it, but for some peculiar, cryptic purpose of his own. He ran, at about fifteen yards' distance from us, right in front of our line of benches, with the aim, perhaps, of reaching the ornamental pond to our left; but before he could do so two chasing attendants closed on him.

Now all this could have been, in one sense, highly comical. But the man's bony, yellowish body, his wide-open mouth as he ran, his shrivelled genitalia bobbing up and down, made you think – I don't know how to put it – of something really terrible, not amusing at all. And this fact seemed to be endorsed by the reactions of the nursing-attendants. As they walked the patient back to his clothes they did not attempt to laugh the matter off. The mood of the sunny afternoon had changed. A third attendant ran up with a blanket to cover the man. They all looked apologetic, ashamed – here where there was so much mental nakedness – as if they had allowed us visitors to witness something unthinkable. And the odd thing was that when I turned back again to Dad, whom I'd almost forgotten in the commotion, he was twisted round on the bench, his arms propped on the back-rest, his head turned away towards the roses so he could not see what was happening.

When Dad and I have sat for some minutes we get up and take a second stroll. This is part of the pantomime too. We walk round the pond and down the yew walk and back over the lawns to the ward. All this time, of course, Dad is utterly silent. As we walk across the trim grass in the hospital grounds I am reminded of how I used to trail behind Dad, lugging his bag of clubs, as a boy, on the golf course at Wimbledon. Every Sunday morning, after an early breakfast; the pigeons clattering out of the hawthorn bushes, the dew still glistening on the fairways. It was one of those gestures of kindness and good will I made only in the period when I had my hamster. I volunteered to be Dad's caddy – no mean feat, when you consider the weight of a loaded golf bag, for a boy of ten. But I used to follow doggedly the little entourage that gathered round Dad at the club-house. They had names – I forget now, Arthur So-and-so, Harry Somebody – and they all had the confi-dent, weathered looks of men who had had, as they used to say then, 'good wars' and become well set-up afterwards. Dad used to make a fuss of me in front of them and they'd tease me in return. Dad was proud of me; he could scarcely credit my new lease of good behaviour, and I don't believe I ever knew him happier than during that time when I had Sammy. What changes that hamster brought about. But what I remember most about those mornings is the 'Wwhack! Wwhack!' of the drivers at the tee; the little jibing, tense remarks that followed, heads tilting to follow the ball; and Dad always getting the best score and no one seeming to mind a bit, as if it were a pleasure to lose to Dad. Dad lifting back his club for the next drive, his body poised, and sweeping it down as if he really meant to punish the little ball, to annihilate it, and the 'Wwhack!' as it struck; and you always knew it would never fail ('Good shot!' and Dad smiles, shielding his eyes); up, up, with a 'whirr' like some flushed game-bird, up, over the gorse and the silver birch and the yellow bunkers, and down again; eighteen times, hounding the ball mercilessly, masterfully, towards the distant flags.

I don't believe Dad will never speak again. It can't be that this awful thing has happened to my father. Sometimes I get the impression that this silence of his is only a pretence, an elaborate, obstinate pretence; that all the time he looks through me and seems not to recognize me, he is really only pretending. The doctors have given him up, but I have a theory that if only I could say the proper things then Dad would answer. Perhaps, with the right words, the right question, I could shock him out of his condition. Perhaps I can ask him questions, now, say things, now, I would never dare utter normally. Like: I respect you Dad, I love you Dad. I looked up to you. I always did, though I never showed it. Why is it my own children don't respect me?

8

During the war my Dad was a spy. He used to be dropped into occupied France and liaise with resistance fighters, keep watch on German installations and help to blow them up. He wrote a book about his exploits, in the fifties, and for a few years his name was well-known, he was one of the war-heroes. He isn't so well-known now – his book's long been out of print – but if you mention his name to people of a certain age, it still rings a dim bell, they know who you mean. Dad was involved in a succession of daring operations in France, which reached their height in the intense period between D-day and the Allied invasion of Germany. It was during this period that he was captured by and subsequently escaped from the Gestapo.

I read Dad's book when it first came out, when I could scarcely have been eleven. It was called *Shuttlecock: The Story of a Secret Agent*. 'Shuttlecock' was Dad's code-name during his final operations in France. I remember that I did not know this word and dared not ask Dad what it meant, and for some time I believed it was a special word invented solely for Father, until one day I found out what a shuttlecock really was: a thing you take swipes at and knock about, like a golf ball. Now I think of it, Dad must have got the idea for writing his book during that same period when I had my hamster. You remember in the early and mid-fifties, when the actual after-effects of the war were fading, rationing was ending, there was a whole spate of war books and war films. He was already sitting up, late at night, in the spare-room-cum-study of our house at Wimbledon, making notes and rough drafts, by the time Sammy died. Perhaps when I next see Dad at the hospital I will say to him: You started *Shuttlecock* because of me, didn't you? Because you and I seemed to be getting on fine.

But the irony of it was I fell away from Dad after I read his book. I'd already been falling away from him after Sammy was chucked into the boiler, but the book clinched it. Oh, it wasn't that I didn't find the book extraordinary, amazing – terrific stuff – that I didn't admire Dad. But, having a hero for a father – even having a father who isn't a hero but who works in a plush office and plays golf on Sundays with a little retinue of worshippers – all this is bad news if you're an only son.

It wasn't that I reverted to how things were before – to flying into fits and biting Dad's hands. But this sullen hostility, this mutual evasion and distrust grew up between us. I gave up being his caddy, for a start (one of those Sunday mornings, Dad at the foot of the stairs: 'Are you coming or not?' Silence – mine. And then the front door slamming and Dad's car revving extra hard outside.) And this was just at the time when Dad was starting to teach me how to use his driver. I made it pretty clear that I didn't care two hoots (I cared, in fact, a good many hoots) about his being a famous spy – even though at certain functions and social gatherings I had to wear (along with Mother, of course, who did it sincerely) a grudging mask of idolatry. When his book came out and reflected glory shone upon me at school I made a point of not bathing in it and of acting as if I found the whole business a bore. So, he blew up ammunition trains? He escaped from the SS? So? And the result of all this, of course, as time wore on, was that Dad gave me up. He ceased to be interested in me as I ceased to be interested in him. When I left school my future had already stopped being a concern of his. When I started in my present job – naturally, I resisted all pressure to become an engineer and to seek an opening in his firm – his reaction was unbridled scorn: 'Police work, eh? *Police* work!' And even when I got married, got a house of my own, had children – *his* grandchildren – he did not unfreeze. He fell back on his life with Mum, and on his work – where, of course, he was still as sprightly and as popular as ever. One particular bone of contention: he has never shown any affection for Marian – not even the attentions due to a daughter-in-law; which I've always resented, because if there was ever any feud, it was between Dad and me only. But Marian and Dad have never been friends; and this became more marked after Mother's death.

When I come home on the Tube in the evening, scanning the rows of faces, reading the adverts for deodorants, hair-transplants and staff agencies, I think it strange that my father was a spy, that he knew adventure, danger, did all those heroic things. I think it even stranger that that same hero is now a human vegetable. His past exploits perhaps mean nothing to him; it's as if it was never he who carried them out. Certainly, he can no longer talk about them.

And maybe that's why I've taken up his book again. There are two copies of it in our house. One has my name in it and 'From your loving Father' in Dad's writing – bold and slanting – and the date, September 1957. Ever since Dad went into his silence I've been poring over it. I must have read it a dozen times, and each time I read it, it seems to get not more familiar but more elusive and remote. There are a thousand questions I want to ask, about things that aren't actually stated in the book. About how Dad *felt* at the time, about what was going on inside him. Because Dad doesn't write about his feelings; he describes events, and where his feelings come into it he conveys them in a bluff, almost light-hearted way, as in some made-up adventure story; so that sometimes this book which is all fact seems to me like fiction, like something that never really took place. What really happened, Dad, at Auxonne? At Combe-les-Dames? What was it like to blow up railways? To hide in a water tank, in four feet of water, all night, while the Gestapo hunted you? To be in constant danger? What was it like when German-hired Cossacks captured one of your comrades and burnt him alive? What was it like, what was it really like?

It's odd that all the time I could have asked him these things, I never did – as if I was never concerned to know the whole truth. And now, when the answers won't come, I want to ask floods of questions. Why is this? It's because for the first time I realize that Dad is *in* that book. He's in there somewhere. It's not some other man, in those pages, with a code-name, Shuttlecock. It's a former consultant engineer, a golf player, a widower, the victim of a mental breakdown. I want to put the two together. Or – put it another way – the book *is* Dad. It's more Dad than that empty effigy I sit beside at the hospital. When I pick it up I still possess Dad, I hold him, even though he's gone away into unbreakable silence. At weekends when Marian talks to her plants I bury myself in Dad's book.

'Chapter Six: With the Maquis Again'.

9

Did I mention, by the way, a little while back, something about taking my kids out on the common at weekends to play healthy games with bats and frisbees? It doesn't really happen, of course. You will have gathered that my relations with Martin and Peter aren't exactly harmonious. Not that we don't go out on the common. But that picture – the exuberant father, the frisky children – it's quite wrong. I have to half drag them along, for a start. I get out my old cricket bat (*my* cricket bat, you notice, from distant school-days – Martin and Peter have never expressed the slightest interest in cricket); or I find the plastic football or the bright red frisbee I bought Peter for his last birthday (a marvellous invention, the sort of thing you'd expect two young boys to play with endlessly and tire out their Dad), and I say: 'Right! We're going to the common. No arguments!'

And what happens? I work up vain enthusiasm. They stubbornly refuse to enter the spirit of the game. They look bored. They want to know what the time is. There is something on television. They moan about being made to run and they argue about who should fetch the ball when, in a spasm of frustration, I take an excessive, but not unpleasing swipe with the bat, which sends it into the distance. They fail to be impressed by or to seek to emulate my expertise with the frisbee (I am very good at the underhand boomerang shot). They look upon me as some sort of demented PT instructor. All this simply isn't natural. And I have to confess another thing. Once, last summer (this is only one of a number of similar instances), when Martin was being particularly troublesome, pretending not to have found one of those knocked-for-six balls, which, when I walked over to him, he suddenly 'spotted' at his feet in the long grass beneath a tree, I had this sudden urge, as he stooped to pick it up, to raise my bat and bring it down, hard, like a club, on the back of his head. I could have done it, I really could.

So we go less and less to the common. Now I wouldn't mind if it was just I who was the obstacle – if Martin and Peter went off to the common to play by themselves – but they don't do this either. And these days it seems that I too, for some inexplicable reason, for some spiteful reason, because what I really want to do is precisely the opposite, am choosing to stay indoors when we could go out.

Today, for instance, is Saturday, the very last day in April. The weather's still fine and warm. It's been exceptionally fine all week. Everything's grown so much in only a few days: the chestnuts on the common, the May trees, the sycamores – but enough of that. Marian slips an arm around me while she makes a morning cup of coffee. I still haven't told her, incidentally, about my promotion.

'Darling, why don't we go out somewhere today after lunch – even before lunch? A picnic? We've done the shopping; there's nothing to stop us. It's the first decent Saturday of the year.'

And almost immediately, because it's Marian who's said it, not me, and even though the very same idea has been crossing my mind since breakfast, I say: 'I don't know. I've got things to do.'

'What things?'

'Oh, odd jobs. This and that.'

Lies, of course. There's nothing I have to do. Though I suddenly see what I *can* do, what I *will* do.

'Well, tomorrow,' Marian says forbearingly. 'If it's still nice.'

'I'm going to see Dad tomorrow.'

Marian looks peevish. This is a sore point. Because I insist on my visits to Dad, we lose days together.

'I thought we might go to Richmond and walk along the river.'

I know why she has said this. It is one of my favourite short outings. There's a pub on the river bank with seats outside where children can sit. Then you can walk along the towpath, upstream, past Ham House, as far as Teddington Lock if you want.

'It'd be nice,' she adds, and gives me a little solicitous look. I know what it means. It means that for some while now she's been noticing there's something on my mind, I'm wound up about something. She daren't ask directly what it is, of course. She knows better than that. But her wisdom tells her what might be a remedy for it: relaxation; air; the sun on the water; dipping willows. You see, Marian is really a very good woman.

'No.' I shake my head. 'But it's all right – you go.'

Now this is a sharp move. It means that Marian must either say, 'Well, I'm not going if you're not coming,' and then we bicker and have a scene; or she really must go without me and run the risk of seeming to neglect me. In the end she plumps (just as I would too) for bold assertion.

'Okay. I will. I'll enjoy it too.'

But now there's an atmosphere of hostility.

'I'll take the car then?' she adds.

'No you won't.'

'Why not?'

'Because you won't take the car, that's why.' (I want the car for my own reasons.)

'Well, how do we get to Richmond?'

'You can take a bus. You've heard about buses? A number 37, all the way. I'll even give you the fare.'

'Thanks.'

She plonks a cup of coffee down in front of me. We might as well have had an all-out scene. But she can still change her mind.

'Won't you come?' she says after a sullen, coffee-sipping pause. The first sign of real weakness.

'No!' I say adamantly.

I go into the living-room, shutting the kitchen door. The boys are lolling about, reading comics. The television is still in the living-room. The boys could switch it on – there are Saturday morning programmes for kids – but they daren't. They know I'd hit them.

I clap my hands, like an animal-trainer. 'Right, you're going out this afternoon, for a walk by the river at Richmond.'

They give me slow, uninterested looks.

'It's all right, I'm not coming. I've got things to do.

You're going with Mum – it's her idea – on the bus.' And almost immediately their eyes, which only a second before had been full of reluctance, begin to show enthusiasm – and relief. This hurts me. Believe me, it does. You see, when I said I didn't mind if it was just I who was the obstacle, that was a lie. What is it that Marian's got that I haven't got? Why do the kids have no axe to grind with Marian?

'Will we go to the pub?' Peter asks.

'No. You're not going till after lunch. But there's a café. I expect you'll get an ice-cream or a drink. If you're good.'

Martin looks up at me resentfully. I fancy that out of the corner of one eye he is glancing slyly towards the television then back to me. That is the difference between Martin and Peter. Peter is the one who got the shaking last Monday, but he has almost forgotten it. Martin is growing up (he will be eleven soon): he bears grudges.

I fish in my pocket. 'Martin, come here.' I pull out four pound notes and when Martin gets up I hold them out to him.

'These are for you. When you get on the bus, you pay for the fares. Don't let Mum pay for anything, understand? And, if there's any change, I want it back.'

'Yes Dad.'

I look into his shifting, sharp little face. He is probably already thinking of ways to pocket the money, or at least hold onto the change. I wonder whether Marian will stand for it, whether it'll make her feel uncomfortable, or whether she'll insist on paying with her own money. And what will Martin do if Marian tells him to keep hold of the money? I look at him. He has cunning, grey-blue eyes under his mop of sandy hair. He's clever enough to understand all this, and to see that I'm testing him.

'Right, put it somewhere safe.'

Later, after lunch, when Marian and the boys have gone, I get down the copy of Dad's book from the shelf in the living-room and start to read it. I read from either of the two copies indiscriminately, picking up whichever is to hand, but naturally the one I value more is the one inscribed by Dad himself. I keep this in our bedroom. That is, usually. For as I sit down now to read the copy from the living-room I discover that at some time or other I have got the two muddled up. The one I have opened has Dad's words in it. '. . . From your loving Father. September 1957.'

I sit down in the armchair by the french windows. The afternoon sun has crept round to shine slant-wise across the garden, and its rays fall obliquely on the glass. The sky is cloudless. I could, of course, sit outside. I look at my watch. It has just turned two. I have about three hours. I could put up a deck-chair on the grass. But I want to feel, though of course it isn't the case at all, that I have been deliberately left behind and forbidden to go out. I want to feel they have gone and left me like some wicked child being punished or some unwanted kill-joy. But what I really want is to read Dad's book.

Dad is in Caen. Caen – 'that testing ground of the future allied advance'. It is six weeks before D-day. He is collecting information on troop movements, supply ship-ments and on the defences of Caen itself, all of which may be of vital importance in the forthcoming invasion. There is a factory in the town which has been turned over to the production of spare parts for divisions on the coast. The details and timing of shipments from the factory have to be known so that effective sabotage can be carried out. This information can only be obtained by gaining access to the supply schedules of the divisions themselves, or more feasibly – but no less hazardously – by secretly examining documents in the office of the factory supervisor.

> . . . I myself volunteered to carry out this task. I knew the lay-out of the factory as well as the others, and the risk was not as great as for Jules and Émile who, after all, would have to stay in Caen and did not have an intelligence network to ferry them out of the area. I learnt how to crack a safe of the type in the *patron*'s office from an old Lyonnais called Maurice, who had been a petty crook in his younger days but was now putting his criminal expertise to patriotic use.
>
> We were fortunate in that the factory was an old, rambling building, slackly guarded, and that the managerial offices, empty at night, occupied an annexe away from the factory itself, across a yard, and abutting other assorted, mostly disused buildings not belonging to the factory complex. They could be approached independently by a roof-top route. The Germans had foolishly expended most of their resources for guarding the factory – sentries, dogs, searchlights – on the factory itself and little on the offices – though it was here that, in the long term, most damage could be done.
>
> Gaining access to the office was to prove a relatively easy part of the operation; but the circumstances of the roof-top route were such that, though an excellent means of approach, it would make an arduous and risky exit. In order to escape from the factory I would have to descend from the office by a back staircase, cross part of

the factory yard and scale a section of the rear factory wall where it turned a convenient corner screening me from the main area of the yard and, so I hoped, the sentries. I was provided with a rope. Jules and Émile were to be waiting, in hiding, near the other side of the wall. When they saw the rope flung over, they were to use it to haul me up the inner side of the wall and, reaching the top, I was to descend on the other side by the simple means of jumping into a sort of cradle formed by their arms – not the most reliable method, but a quick one and one we had practised several times before.

Success rested on the reported laxity of the guards, and a good measure of luck. These were urgent days, when there was no time for delay or finesse. We could no longer rely on the RAF to ease our work – they were now reluctant to concentrate raids in Normandy for fear of giving away future invasion sites. Every opportunity we failed to take through too much caution might take its toll on the effectiveness of that future invasion.

The night we chose was that of May 2nd. A warm night; patchy clouds; a faint moon. I parted from my comrades and slipped, some minutes later, into the narrow streets which led to my roof-top route. I carried the rope, coiled tightly round my waist, a plan of the factory in my head, and a knife. I remember that as I made my way I had the strange sensation of being no more than an ordinary burglar. My forebodings about what lay ahead were curiously like those of a civilian lawbreaker – as if I feared discovery by the police rather than the enemy. I have sometimes wondered whether this was a feeling peculiar to the undercover agent – without his absolving uniform – the feeling of being less a spy than a criminal. In his role, war and peace-time get confused. Do civilized instincts persist in war, or does civilized life veil the instincts of war? I cannot say. On that May night I had little time for philosophiz-ing . . .

And it's that last passage, along with barely a handful of others like it, which, lately, I've been reading and rereading and which I've marked already, in both copies, in pencil. Those rare betrayals of feeling; those rare moments of self-scrutiny, of speculation. All so quickly dismissed. 'I cannot say.' I stare at the page. I read the words as though, if I read hard enough, other words will appear: Dad will begin to speak.

I glance at my watch. Five to three. People strolling along the river path at Richmond. The first decent Saturday of the year. Marian; and the kids. On the river, passing pleasure boats and launches. A swan, with a bevy of fraught cygnets, riding the wash.

. . . things had gone so well up to this point that I almost anticipated trouble in the later stages. I descended the rear fire-escape stairs from the corridor adjoining the *patron*'s office. This brought me out into a cobbled passage-way, between two office blocks, one end blind and the other opening out on to the part of the yard I had to cross – or rather skirt, keeping to whatever shadow I could find. My position was now essentially that of the escaper from a walled prison. I had transferred my coil of rope to my shoulder, in readiness in case things came to a quick dash.

I started forward along the passage-way. I had gone a few paces and was a short distance from the yard when a sentry appeared in the opening, halted, in a stooping, unsoldierly fashion and stood with his back towards me. How he failed to see me, I don't know. As he turned, he must have looked, even if inadvertently, down the passage-way, and I would not have said that, at that range, the shadows were enough to hide me. I could only freeze, my heart pounding, against the wall. The sentry tugged at his rifle sling, easing it on his shoulder, and then his hands seemed to be busy at his pockets: the unmistakable actions of a man preparing to light a cigarette. It was likely he would choose the concealment of the passage-way in which to smoke: five minutes on tenterhooks.

Experience had taught me that where there is a choice between several possibilities which cannot be calculated exactly, and cold steel, then cold steel is the better choice. At all events, decision is better than hesitation. The sentry might smoke his cigarette and move on, and I might wait for him – though I would still have his presence to contend with. On the other hand, he might turn his head at any moment. If I silenced him, and even if I eventually got out of the factory successfully, our break-in would naturally be discovered, and the Germans, if they had any sense, would switch the schedules of their shipments. But then again, since everything in the office had been left as I found it, there was just a chance they would take the death of the sentry to mean a sabotage attempt on the factory itself, search the premises for explosives, and overlook the information in the *patron*'s office. Better this chance than my capture and outright failure.

All this must have passed through my brain in seconds. But a simple fact tipped the scales in favour of cold steel. The German was standing, reaching for his cigarette, not inside the passageway, but just beyond its entrance, in view of the yard. This meant that he must himself be unobserved and that he was presumably confident he would remain so for the length of time it took him to enjoy his illicit cigarette. If I acted at once I could take advantage of the safety he himself had indicated to me.

The stiletto I had acquired at Tarbes was in its sheath inside my trousers against my hip. It could be drawn almost noiselessly, but I took the precaution of waiting for a masking sound – the German striking his match. The match flared. I drew the stiletto. The German's head bent into his cupped hands, the flame lighting up his helmet and a thin strip of neck above his collar. I moved a step or two forward along the wall. I knew that if the Germans found a dead guard they would take reprisals, and, for want of anyone else, they might shoot one or two of the innocent factory workers. But I could already hear Jules' and Émile's laconic response. 'N'importe' – my friends would spit – 'they shouldn't make parts for the Boches.'

I took another step forward. If the sentry should turn round now to throw his match into the passage-way, better he should come face to face with me with my drawn stiletto than catch me at a distance. But he tossed the match casually to his right, scarcely moving his head. As his right hand was engaged, returning the match-box to his pocket, I struck – my left hand covering his mouth, fingers pinching the nose, the blade entering left of the spine: a text-book application of my close combat training. The only thing I had forgotten was the cigarette. My hand rammed most of it into the sentry's mouth, but I was left with an angry burn in the centre of my palm . . .

My Dad. Cold steel. A man's back.

Marian and the kids are walking through the gardens, opposite the ice rink; round the bend where the river stretches away upstream in a long, straight, tree-fringed view; on, along the towpath by Petersham meadows, where there are always some cows or a pony or two; the boys will walk along the top of the little concrete wall by the towpath, as they always do, and Marian will walk below. Then to the ferry point at River Lane, where the trees begin – the tall chestnuts behind the towpath, in new leaf, and, by the river, alders and willows, dipping and stooping over the water, the wash heaving over the branches, scooting mallards . . . I can see all this almost more vividly than if I were there myself. And suddenly I clutch Dad's book closer, protectively, to me, as if Marian, likewise, can see me with it, sitting by the french windows, like a man with a secret no one else must see, with a possession no one else must share.

. . . Reprisals did take place. We heard that two men from the factory were questioned then arbitrarily shot. But the shipment times were not changed. One shipment – the next scheduled that month – was successfully sabotaged, not by our group but by Lucien's. Following this, we heard that the factory manager was being 'investigated' by the Gestapo.

But it was now time for me to bid adieu to Jules and Émile. My period in the Caen region was coming to an end . . .

So Dad slips away (end of Chapter 12), terse and brisk as ever, to his next assignment; to be picked up, in a moonlit field, by an RAF Lysander; to be dropped, four weeks later, into France again. And so he slips away from me; into the realms of action and iron nerves; into the silence of a man on a hospital bench. That one moment of reflection, of perplexity. What was it like, Dad? What was it like to be brave and strong?

At the end of River Lane there are usually parked cars; an ice-cream van. Marian will stop here. Will Martin pay? I am saying these things as if somehow the statement of them is something more than the reality. Like Dad's book – like these jottings of mine, which are fast turning into a book too. The smell of the river: a mixture of mud, oil and sodden timber. Why aren't I there? Martin and Peter lick their ice-creams. Marian licks hers. Or perhaps she doesn't have one. She has this thing about keeping her figure – I approve of it – though she isn't in the least overweight. The kids go down to the river's edge, where the water laps at the slipway. Some dinghies are pulled up. Marian stays up on the bank, watching them. But she isn't really thinking of them, I know. As she stands on the bank, her eyes dim and a half-guilty, half-mystified look crosses her face. She is thinking of me.

On, further; along the towpath, bushes and trees now on either side. The sun flickering through the willow stems. The boys walking ahead, looking for large sticks to brandish, Marian walking behind, a little abstractedly. Into the grounds of Ham House. Across the trim lawns; tulips and gravel walks (now *there* is a similarity I have never thought of – the grounds of Ham House and the grounds of Dad's mental hospital). They say the first occupant of Ham House – a cabinet minister of Charles II – was half mad. Once we took the boys to look round the inside of the house; they were bored, and afterwards I lectured them on the importance of a sense of history (you see, I am not only cowardly, but pompous too) . . . Into the gardens at the back of the house where the tea shop is. And there, while she watches the sparrows peck at crumbs, the same anxious look will cross her face.

All of this touches me more than if I were really there to see it happen.

Four-fifteen. Dad leaps from a Halifax bomber into the Haute-Saône.

Have I mentioned yet how Marian and the kids behave on the subject of Dad? They are quite heartless about him. They forget about him. Marian once skipped halfheartedly through Dad's book; but the kids have never read it. They don't visit him; they don't think of him as my father so much as a peculiar object I go and see on certain Wednesdays and Sundays. (I took the boys to visit Dad once: I said, 'Martin and Peter, Dad, your grandsons,' but Dad didn't move an eyelid and the boys giggled, and afterwards they started to talk about 'Grandpa Loony' – as opposed to Grandpa Lenny, who is Marian's father, and, of course, perfectly *compos mentis*.) When I come back from visiting Dad, Marian never says, 'How is he?' or 'Any better?' She blames me for going in the first place. She blames me for repeatedly going on these pointless trips. She blames Dad for being a liability and she blames me for Dad's being blameworthy. And she communicates this blame to the kids. I have even noticed that she sometimes fails to upbraid them when they talk about 'Grandpa Loony'. I know what they are all thinking when I go off to see Dad every Wednesday or Sunday: they are thinking I go there just to get away from them.

Four-fifteen. I don't have much time. I return Dad's book to the shelf. I disconnect the television, carry it out to our car, and drive to the rental shop.

10

It was about three months after Dad's breakdown that I first began to suspect that something strange was happening at work. I remember I had been to the hospital one Sunday afternoon. The doctor was there – Doctor Townsend, a tall, angular man with a breezy manner and glasses – and after my 'chat' with Dad he wanted to see me. He walked with me down the hospital drive to the gates, his tie flapping out of his white coat. 'It's been nearly two months, Mr Prentis ... I have to be frank with you ... We've made virtually no progress...' He held out a hand, as though to clasp my shoulder, but merely held it poised in the air. 'There's always a possibility – a remote one – that something you may say may succeed ... Don't give up, Mr Prentis,' – he twisted the corner of his mouth into a smile – 'the key might lie with you.'

And then, on the Monday morning, Quinn handed me the first of those inquiry dossiers, which he has been handing me from time to time ever since, in which the items have scarcely anything in common and seem to lead nowhere.

You may well ask, as this was the very first instance,

why didn't I simply take the matter up with Quinn? That is not such a simple question, and it begs the further one of my relations with Quinn. They had taken some odd turns in the weeks after Dad's breakdown. I have said already that the first time I have known Quinn to be pleasant to me was last Monday when he mentioned my promotion. That was something of an exaggeration, I admit – though that's not to say that pleasantness from Quinn isn't a rarity. However, there was one brief occasion when Quinn was not only pleasant but positively sympathetic – and that was over the business of Dad.

It's true, I never meant to ask for compassionate leave. I meant to soldier on and not even mention at the office that my Dad, a vigorous, active man in his fifties, had become a silent wreck. I meant to bear it nobly. I thought of how Dad himself had soldiered on, after Mum's death ... But then – how do I begin to describe the shock of Dad's breakdown? The misery of that evening when Marian and I rushed to the hospital and were shown this stranger lying drugged in a bed. No more scorn for my 'police work'; no more cold-shouldering of Marian. An empty stare. That night I lay awake (Marian went fast to sleep – she dropped off, just like that, with her father-in-law lying in hospital). I got up and smoked a packet of cigarettes. I thought to myself: now it is your turn to be strong. But all the time the question kept repeating itself, like a little wave inside my skull: Why? Why?

And then in the Tube the next morning – you see the effect the Tube has – I gave in. My fellow passengers would have had their satisfaction that day – they'd have seen a man with his defences down. The first thing I did when I got into work was to go and see Quinn. And he was all understanding. 'My dear chap – I'm so sorry. Yes, have the rest of the week off – take as much time as you like.' He made me sit down. He sat opposite me in his leather chair. And I couldn't help thinking that Dad had been found, the day before in his office, in his leather chair, which was bigger even than Quinn's. There was a moment – just as I began to explain things – when Quinn's eyes seemed to sharpen and brighten a little, like a doctor's, who while he is listening to you describe your symptoms, suddenly becomes interested in your appearance, in the *way* you are talking. But his manner, like a good doctor's too, was considerate and patient. I actually felt grateful for his concern (what sympathy could I get from Marian, who had never had any for Dad?). And, to tell you the truth, all that 'dear chapping' and 'dear fellowing', which in its old-fashioned way, might have been just glib lip-service, that comforted me more than anything. It made me think of the suave, chummy talk I used to hear outside the clubhouse when Dad and his friends came in from their golf for their drinks . . .

But what happened after this? I took the rest of that week off. After my return to work, Quinn inquired every so often, in a perfectly friendly manner, after Dad. The ice was breaking; I seemed to have found favour. But then – after several weeks – his attitude began suddenly to harden. It was not just that he returned to his old self again; he became more severe, more tyrannical than ever before. The subject of Dad got dropped altogether; it became a sort of taboo. It was during this time that I began positively to feel that there was an evil streak in Quinn and it was directed specifically at me. Was all this a delusion brought about by my own unsettled state of mind? Or was it a consequence I ought to have foreseen? Had I made a mistake in letting Quinn peep so far into my private life? Wasn't this just the sort of thing a man like him would seize upon? Had I been taken in by all those words of consolation and that plump, dimpled face – like the face of some complacent abbot?

I only knew that something odd was going on, and when that first jumbled dossier arrived on my desk, my immediate instinct was one of caution. All right, call it cowardice if you like. What if Quinn were baiting me? What if he were trying to tempt me into some hasty assumption that would catch me out? I responded judiciously. I pretended to chase up the contents of the files – or rather I genuinely looked for some hidden meaning behind the unrelated items. I wrote at the end of a rather garbled report: 'the evidence is fragmentary and justifies no significant conclusions' (my pompous style again) and I returned it to Quinn. No comment. But when, after another three weeks or so, I received a second dossier of a similar kind, I knew this was not a matter of some chance error or quirk. I began to think twice about the files I had already occasionally, but without leaping to any con-clusions, found missing, but which now I felt must be obscurely connected with these strange dossiers. Quinn was up to something. Perhaps it involved the whole depart-ment. But why was Quinn, as it were, letting me know about it? Why was he daring me to enter in on it – or expose it? I looked around at my colleagues for any signs that their suspicions had also been aroused or that they had been given similar inquiries to work on. But the papers I sometimes surreptitiously leafed through on their desks, their unchanged, unconstrained chatter in the pub at lunch-times, made me sure that I was alone. I began to draw apart from them at this time – from Vic and Eric, with whom I used to discuss marital ups and downs, plans for summer holidays – and no doubt they noticed it. But they knew vaguely what had happened to Dad and they put my reserve down to that.

I handled the second dossier in the same way as the first. I spread the items out on my desk and pretended to be engrossed. But I remember that while I was 'busy' at it I looked up once, and there was Quinn, at his glass panel, staring down, not at our office at large, but directly at me. He was wearing a black pin-stripe, with a small flower – a little pale yellow rose – in his lapel. I'd never seen Quinn wear a flower before; he wasn't the sort of man to wear flowers – though quite often, after this, I noticed he wore one. When I looked up he didn't even turn his head away till some seconds had passed. He had a fascinated look on his face; and I'd swear he was simply relishing my perplexity.

And another thing. It was at this time too that the rumour got around – it was one of those rumours that come down slowly from high places; it wasn't given out by Quinn himself, though he never denied it – that Quinn would be retiring the next summer but one, when, so we learnt, he would be sixty-four. This was a new retirement scheme to allow fresh staff into higher positions. Quinn still had the option of working on till sixty-five – or even longer – if he wished. Naturally, I had an interest in this. There was a chance – a very slim and remote one – that I might be offered Quinn's job, but this would depend almost entirely on Quinn's own recommendation. I was now in the quandary which I have described already. If

I challenged Quinn over the mysterious goings-on in the office, would that instantly ruin my promotion chances? Should I hold my tongue and knuckle under? Or was it conceivable that those mysterious goings-on (one couldn't deny how they coincided with the retirement rumours) were some elaborate test of my initiative: if I *didn't* take some stand about them would I then wreck my chances? And yet again, didn't my duty lie outside the whole self-interested field of my promotion prospects? If I suspected something untoward in the department, shouldn't I act promptly to denounce it? You hear about corruption in official places – about mismanagement, leaks of information. You hear all sorts of stories.

Would I be writing all this down now, trying to clarify matters in words, if I had acted on any of these assumptions? No. The question of Quinn's retirement only added to my existing confusion. Sometimes – usually in that brief, green breathing-space on my way home, between the Underground station and our house – I would reflect that, in the possibility of exposing single-handedly some malpractice in the office, lay the opportunity of bringing into my life a faint note of daring, decision – integrity. But then, supposing my gamble failed? And I *wanted* that promotion. I wanted to come home one day and say to Marian and the kids: I've got a better job, an important job, I'll be better now. (Look what I actually did when Quinn broke the news.) And then it would strike me that there were really two promotions I wanted. For, quite apart from prospects at work, I wanted to step into Dad's shoes. Now his mind was gone, now Dad was no more: I wanted what he had had. To be even with him. And then there was Quinn. Now and then in the office, when I came into contact with him, I would seethe inwardly with a mixture of hatred, envy and a desire for certainty. I wanted his job. I wanted to sit in his leather chair. I wanted to look down, like him, through his glass panel, at the underlings I had once worked beside. And yet it seemed (and I still feel this now) that what I wanted was not so much the promotion itself, but to be in a position where I would *know*; where I would no longer be the victim, the dupe, no longer be in the dark.

And when all is said – does this sound strange? – I didn't want to hurt Quinn. I didn't want any action of mine to topple him, to break him.

One Sunday when all this was preying on my mind, I went to see Dad – and my patience ran out. 'All right,' I said, 'let's stop playing shall we?' My voice was raised. We were sitting on the bench under the cedar within earshot of other people – but in that place my shouts would probably have been taken for the babblings of just another lunatic. 'What's the matter with you?' I said. 'Why don't you tell me? Why don't you speak?' As if Dad were deliberately deceiving me. 'What's it all about?' Then I suddenly yelled: 'I hate you!' All the time he looked straight before him, his face never flickered, and little midges were jigging in the air under the cedar. And I realized I was talking to Dad as if I were talking to Quinn.

11

Marian and I make love, on average, three or four times a week. It is rare for her to make excuses; to say that she has the proverbial headache or that she has forgotten her doo-dah as she did recently – and as she attempted again last night, after discovering that I really had returned the television to the shop. She has learnt by now to submit to my demands. There have sometimes passed whole weeks, hectic and fatiguing weeks, in which every night we have striven to cap the passion of the night before. The reason for this intensity is not really mutual ardour, or any excess of appetite on my part – and perhaps passion is the wrong word. It has more to do with my constant dissatisfaction.

You see – (but now I'm going to speak about very intimate things, very private things – never mind, I let myself in for it when I began these pages) – it's a long time since I've experienced with Marian that thing called 'ecstasy' or 'fulfilment'. Believe me, it's that that I'm looking for – not some mere superficial thrill – when we labour away in the dark, or, more often, with the lights on so we can see what we're doing when we twist ourselves into some untried, contortionate position. Often, I have spent whole afternoons at the office, ostensibly busy with my paper-work, in reality anticipating, planning in meticulous detail our activities of the night. And when I started to buy certain 'manuals', to get Marian to send off for certain articles from catalogues, to visit the sex shops in Charing Cross Road and Leicester Square, all this paraphernalia wasn't an end in itself, believe me, it was all in the hope of achieving some ultimate thing that always seemed elusive.

Making love ought to be the most natural thing, oughtn't it? This week, in the full flush of spring, I have been watching the sparrows copulating on our guttering – a mere hop and then it's over – and the ducks – more rapacious – on the common. It is so simple. Nature prompts them when the season comes, and – I don't mind admitting it – I often envy their easy contentment, not to be constantly at it, the whole year through. They don't need any fetishist tricks to urge them on or any shame to restrain them. And sometimes that is just how I see it with Marian and me: a little careless, unadorned instant, like the sparrows; a little flutter of wings and hearts: at one with nature. Perhaps it was like that once, long ago. For Marian and me. For all of us. But now we have to go through the most elaborate charades, the most strenuous performances to receive enlightenment. Because that is the goal, don't mistake me – enlightenment. All nature's creatures join to express nature's purpose. Somewhere in their mounting and mating, rutting and butting is the very secret of nature itself. And when, night after night, I conduct my sexual experiments with Marian, for ever modifying the formula, it's with the yearning that one day it won't just be sex, but enlightenment.

Marian sometimes says I'm hurting her; or 'Can't we do it another way?' or 'Couldn't we stop now – wait till the morning?' And sometimes it's less my physical insistence that wears her than my demands for things she's quite unable to supply. For example, sometimes I wish Marian had bigger breasts. Her breasts, I may say, are petite and compact, and perfectly lovely in their way. But sometimes I want her to have big, blouse-bursting tits like Maureen's in the typing pool. Once, so rumour has it, Eric got Maureen into the stationery cupboard and induced her, as part of some bet, to let him see what they were like. And I'm not sure that things stopped at that. Marian can't be expected to satisfy my fantasies about a girl she hasn't even seen. But I demand it nonetheless (without mentioning Maureen of course), and I have even given Marian (who worries about her waistline) a complex about the size of her bust.

All in all, I'm surprised how little she resists. (Her wonderful pliancy.) She's afraid, of course, of what might happen if she did. But then one reason why I think she complies is that she shares the adventure. Yes, adventure – why not use that word? It's not a misplaced one for what Marian and I get up to in our bedroom. I read somewhere once in a magazine – it was one of Marian's magazines – that sexual adventure is the only form of adventure left to us in our age. It compensates for all the excitement and initiative we've lost in other ways. The only true revolution now is sexual revolution, and that is why everything – look around – is becoming increasingly, visibly oriented to sex. Well, if sex is the only true revolution, I don't see why Marian and I shouldn't play our part. I'm not extremist, after all – I'm not a promiscuous man – I'm just an ordinary rebel. Though, sometimes – quite often, of late, to tell you the truth – I have these reactionary moods. Sometimes, coming home on the Tube to Marian, stimulated by the adverts and the proximity of knots of office girls, I wonder: if it's all so visible and acceptable, and the magazines tell you to do it – what's so rebellious about it?

All right, so you've gathered it by now. My sex-life is really a preposterous, an obsessive, a pathetic affair. A sham, a mockery. Systematically and cold-bloodedly, like a torturer bent on breaking his victim, I am turning my wife into a whore. This same woman who goes, dutifully, to collect our kids from school; who takes them for walks in the sunshine along the Thames. (By the way, Martin gave her the four pounds but she never spent it; and when she came back she said, in Martin's presence: 'There's the money you gave to Martin to give to me.' Conspirators!)

Tell me, can a man do wrong with his own wife? And are there really crimes, rights and wrongs, in those areas of our lives – you know what I mean – where we are like lost explorers, and right and wrong, with the rest of civilization, have been left behind at the base camp? All my relentless demands on Marian, don't they all mean, underneath, that I *want* Marian, that Marian is very dear to me? I've never wanted another woman since we married – that's the honest truth. (All right, *bits* of other women.) And isn't it possible that this whole voluntary confession (I never dreamed I would be setting down things like this) is inspired by some upsurge of guilt where guilt should not apply, and that I over-sensitively exaggerate what I suppose to be the shamefulness of my proclivities? What is healthy and normal in this sphere, after all?

Actually, to cut all this shilly-shally, what really fills me with dread is something else. It is the thought that, one day, by some mischance, Martin and Peter might stumble upon me and Marian in some posture impossible to explain, even to a boy who has an inkling (and I'm sure Martin has more than that) of what Mummies and Daddies do after bed-time. And that in an instant whatever trust, whatever shred of faith they had in their father will vanish. What would they say – princes brought up in the security of the castle, suddenly discovering the dungeons? What would *I* say – groping for the blankets? 'Now children, all this is normal.'

No. Please.

And it's an odd thing that I've brought the children in at this point. Because all this assault-course sex with Marian, all this feverish searching for erotic illumination – it only began with the kids being born. Or, rather, not with them being born exactly – because do you know what I felt when each of them came into the world? I felt: life is very simple and complete. And there was a time even when the boys were small, when Marian and I used to make love, quite spontaneously, in the open air – in fields, amid ferns, in secluded parts of beaches – when we went out at weekends. Martin nestling close by, asleep in the carry-cot. No, it wasn't with their being born but with their growing up – with the idea that they will one day be men like me. The older they get, the more persistent, the more desperate I become with Marian. When will their growing, I wonder, outstrip my libido? Or will I have found, before then, what it is I'm seeking?

One day when I go to see Dad I will say to him: Is it

wrong, the way I treat Marian? You and Mum were always the fine, confident couple. If you were such a hero, did you always have good, healthy relations with your wife? Even bed-time ones? Tell me, Dad. Enlighten me.

12

It is now several days since I returned the television to the shop. They all resent me for it – I can see that – but apart from one barbed remark from Marian when they came back from their afternoon at Richmond ('I suppose you think that was clever. Happy now?'), there have been no demonstrations. They're shrewd enough, I imagine, not to give me the opportunity to crow – 'No idle threats from me, you see,' or something of the kind. By Monday the whole matter seemed to have died down, though the week began sullenly enough and Martin, in particular, kept giving me little hard, vengeful frowns.

But today (Friday) – though it really began yesterday – something has happened. Something I can't help taking very seriously.

The weather has kept up all the week. It seems we are in for a remarkable summer. I have come home, sticky from the Tube and enervated from work, but with enough vigour to muster, on my arrival, a mocking heartiness. 'Well, who's for a game of cricket on the common?' Now the television has gone it seems only proper to take the initiative over healthier, alternative activities. But, as is to be expected, my proposal meets with wilful non-enthusiasm. 'Suit yourselves then.' In order to endorse my position, I have often thought of going out alone, not to play cricket, of course, but for solitary strolls across the common. I might even have a self-righteous pint or two at the pub. But in fact, as you know now, I have been more occupied by something else which both the absence of the television and, indirectly, the warm weather have made more feasible. Every evening this week, before and after supper, I have been taking the copy of *Shuttlecock* from the shelf in the living-room, setting up a deck-chair in the garden and in stubborn indifference to my family, following Dad across occupied France.

Until yesterday, that is, when I came home to find that the copy of the book was gone.

Now I did not act in haste. I checked in my memory that I had actually returned it to the shelf the previous night; I looked elsewhere in the living-room; I made sure it had not been put with the other copy in the bedroom; I asked Marian if she knew its whereabouts; I paused to size the situation. Only then did I jump to conclusions. Martin, Martin. A reprisal.

'Martin,' (with feigned casualness), 'have you seen my book?'

'What book?'

'You know. Grandpa's book.'

'Haven't seen it.'

'Martin, tell me what you have done with it.'

'Nothing. I haven't done anything.'

His face had an expression of grim tenacity, which was confession enough.

'Martin, don't play tricks with me. Tell me where it is.'

'How should I know.'

'Where?!!'

And then anger got the better of me. If my subsequent course of action seems excessive, remember that it was the *signed* copy ('your loving Father') that was missing. Had it been the other copy – you must believe me – I would not have felt half my rage.

With my left hand I seized Martin's right arm and twisted it behind his back in a sort of imperfect half-nelson. I raised my right hand into a position to strike him across the face.

'Now! Are you going to tell me?'

We were standing in the living-room. As the shouting began, Marian appeared in the doorway, and out of the corner of my eye I noticed that Peter, who had been in the garden and who may or may not have been in on the theft of the book, had come to the french windows and was watching apprehensively to see how his brother would shape up. Given my superior strength and the way the sympathies of the family stood, everything favoured Martin being the hero of the moment.

'I'm going to count to three.'

It struck me momentarily that this confrontation, in all its crudity, was really little different from the sort of set-tos that are commonplace in school playgrounds. This being the case, Martin probably had the advantage in immediate experience; for, despite their unadventurousness at home, I often noticed (it used to puzzle me) that both he and Peter returned from school with cuts and bruises that suggested scraps on the asphalt.

'One – '

I jerked his left arm and lifted my right hand a little

further. Martin gasped and turned his head to one side. His little face became grimmer still.

Marian stepped forward. 'If you hurt him, I'll – '

'You'll what?'

She put a hand out to stop mine. I raised mine still further. I wondered briefly whether to strike Martin or Marian. Martin's eyes were screwed up, waiting for the blow. I have to admit that everything was blurred and strange. I had a vision of how families fall apart, of how terrible crimes get committed in ordinary circumstances

'All right,' I said, dropping Martin's arm. 'I don't have to hit you.'

Instantly, Martin opened his eyes and turned in innocent appeal to Marian. 'I don't know anything about it, Mum.' So well acted.

'We'll see about that,' I said. I pushed past the two of them into the hall and bounded up the stairs to the boys' bedroom. I looked under Martin's bed and under Peter's bed. Opened their clothes drawers. I checked their own bookshelves, taking in the titles: *Pioneers of Space*; *The Martian Menace*: *Miracles of the Laser*. On the wall was an absurd picture of Telly Savalas sucking a lollipop; a faded chart showing details of all the Apollo moonflights. I pulled open the doors to the cupboard in which were stored the accumulated toys of half a decade, and out spilled a tangled mass of gadgetry – ray-guns, limbless action-men, scale models of rockets and lunar modules, a broken pocket-calculator, ribbons of shiny cassette-tape: a cybernetical junkyard. Nothing simple and down-to-earth – like a cricket bat. And no copy of Dad's book.

I was beginning to consider that I might be wrong in

my suspicions, but it was too late to call off the performance.

I went down to the living-room.

'Well,' I said reflectively, like an inquisitor considering that direct violence may not be the best ploy. 'There are other ways of getting it out of you.'

I looked quickly at Marian.

'Are you hungry, Martin?'

I should explain that every weekday the boys have a large tea at about four-thirty, after they come in from school. Until recently this used to be their last main meal of the day and Marian and I used to have a separate supper at about seven. In recent months, however, with the boys staying up later and later (because of that damned television) and demanding 'pre-bedtime snacks', we have shifted towards their eating regularly with us. They are growing boys with massive appetites. The upshot is that they now have both a large tea when they come in and a large supper a couple of hours later.

'You don't get anything to eat until you tell me where that book is. Understand? Not tonight, not tomorrow, not – '

'For goodness' sake!' Marian said.

'I mean what I say. Martin only has to own up.'

'But how do you – ?'

'I know. Books don't just disappear from shelves. Have you got a better explanation?'

About half an hour after this we had supper. I made Martin stand with his face to the wall like a naughty boy in class. I wasn't going to give him even the partial respite of not being present while we ate. I made a point of asking for large helpings. Peter picked and spooned guiltily at his plate. Sometimes Peter is so tremulous, so mouse-like. I watched Martin. He didn't turn his head. The backs of his thin legs beneath his shorts wobbled now and then, and I remembered the flavour of childhood punishments: the humiliation, the obscurity of adult motives; the vague feeling of outlawdom; the determination to resist. I did not expect him to own up that evening. In a strange way, I would almost have been disappointed if he had. He had had his tea, after all, and was probably too on edge at the moment to care about the loss of food. But the night would see to it. In the morning, I told myself, in the morning he will break.

At breakfast I followed the same procedure. Martin stood in the corner. He had adopted a martyrish pose which seemed to me wholly contrived. I noticed that he moved his head this time, in a quite deliberate way, as if designed for me to see, though not towards us so much as towards the front window beyond our breakfast table. It was another sunny day; between the cherry blossoms a council dust-cart was grinding down the road. Marian and I were silent with each other. I made a song and dance about enjoying my bacon and eggs. But as the minutes passed, as it drew nearer to the time when I must leave for work, I grew anxious. I knew that the boys left the house about a quarter of an hour after I did. In that quarter of an hour not only might Marian have time to shovel a hasty breakfast down Martin, but she would doubtless pack him off to school, coddled and consoled, with double rations of sandwiches. Martin knew this too. I considered whether it was worth being late to work in order not to lose the battle.

I finished my cup of coffee and got up from the table.

'Right,' I said. 'Now, are you going to tell me? I don't have to rush to work. It's your last chance. You can turn round now.'

Martin turned. He looked ruefully for some time at his feet and then up, deliberately again, at me.

'All right.'

'At last! Good boy!' I really was relieved, glad – no longer vindictive.

'I threw it in the dustbin.' He cocked his head towards the window. The dust-cart had departed from the street. 'It will have gone by now.'

'You what?' I said, advancing across the floor. 'You what?!'

He pressed his lips together. His face tautened.

'That was my book!' With a genuine woundedness in my voice. 'That was Grandpa's book!'

'Grandpa – '

He didn't have time to say more before the first slap caught him across the face. Then another. And another. The extraordinary thing was that he didn't turn or duck away. His feet remained firmly planted on the carpet. It was as if he had bargained all along on these blows. Tears of shock rather than fright or pain filled his eyes, but he kept his head erect and his shoulders square, like a soldier looking to the front while the sergeant screams in his ear. Even as I hit him I couldn't help but grudgingly admire him; and it was this, rather than Marian tugging at my other arm, that made me stop.

When I did, Martin simple turned, and without hurrying, without clapping his hands to his smarting cheeks or breaking into sobs, walked from the room. I sat down again at the table. I was going to be late for work now. I looked at Peter and Marian, who, surprised as I was at Martin's self-control, had not rushed out immediately to comfort him.

'Well, he deserved it, didn't he? He stole my book.'

I was puffed – and petulant – from my exertions.

Marian looked at me in furious silence, then pushed back her chair and turned to leave the room. But she was scarcely on her feet before the door opened and Martin entered carrying a book. He walked towards me with an air of precarious dignity and put the book on the table.

'You hit me for nothing, Dad. Nothing at all. I never threw it away.'

I looked at him. Then at the book. I opened it at the flyleaf: there was Dad's writing. 'Your loving . . .' I looked at Martin again for several seconds. At the book.

The jacket of the original edition has the picture of a man, in silhouette, dangling from an opening parachute. For the first time I seemed to see the terrible vulnerability of this position, and the attempt of the artist to make the image resemble a shuttlecock.

'Why did you – ?' I started fiercely. But my anger had spent itself. 'Why did you take it?'

'Because you took away the television.'

And I suppose, I thought, you want me to follow your example and bring it back.

'I see. The television didn't belong to you though, did it?'

But I knew we weren't talking about just the television. I looked into his face. His cheeks were bright pink from the slapping he'd had. I thought of the cunning with which he must have planned this little operation, and the guile and resolution with which he had carried it out. Those glances out of the window; the readiness to go hungry, to provoke and endure punishment. He was brave, he was resourceful, all right. He was his grandfather's grandson. His eyes bored into me. How much did he understand?

'If someone takes something from you – even *if* that was wrong of them – it's no answer to take something from them,' I said feebly.

He nodded, uncontrite.

No, not just the television; but all that went with the television. The Bionic Man and Kojak and Captain Kirk, and all the other made-up heroes who were better than his father. For some unaccountable reason I felt in awe of my own son, as if I should make things up to him, beg his mercy, but I was unable – unworthy – to do so.

I was going to be very late for work.

'Martin,' I said. 'All this was stupid, wasn't it? Why did you do it?' Then I added suddenly: 'Why haven't you ever read Grandpa's book? You wouldn't find it difficult.'

He shook his head – as if sorry for me. I knew he would never read the book. And I understood, too, his complex reasons – part suspicion and contempt, and part some nagging child's fear (only now did I see it), all of which might have been expressed, and at that very moment, in one word: Loony.

13

Today (Monday) it struck me that Quinn could be invent-
ing everything. Those inquiries. Supposing they are all in
some extraordinary way figments of his imagination? How
am I to know what's true and what isn't and what really
stems from an official directive? Supposing he sits in his
office picking out file numbers at random, adds a few fancy
details of his own; has it all drawn up by a typist, who'd
be none the wiser, on an instruction sheet, and then
hands it on to me as part of some sadistic trick? It sounds
far-fetched, I know – but if Quinn were really round the
bend – ?

He called me in today. I thought he was going to speak
again of my promotion – it is two weeks now since the
subject was first mentioned – but he didn't; though I could
see him reading my expectations and playing with my
hopes.

'C9, Prentis, C9. I've been looking over your report.
There's nothing here about the past histories of X or Z'
(the blackmailer and the second civil servant). 'If we're
trying to establish a connexion between the two, I would
have thought that was the first thing to look at. Black-

mailers don't operate by chance – you have to discover the link in the past, the common ground.'

'With respect, sir,' (how I hate that phrase, 'with respect'), 'I didn't know that was the reason for the inquiry.'

'Is that so, Prentis? You mean it never crossed your mind?'

'As a possibility, yes sir. But doesn't the evidence point towards a coincidence – a curious one – but nothing more?' I hastily recalled the C9 inquiry, a pattern in which there were large holes and gaps where items were missing from the files – so perhaps not a pattern at all. 'Y was fully exonerated. X's circumstances – his previous sacking, alcoholism and so forth – all suggest malicious slander, not calculated blackmail. There is no apparent link between Y and Z. And, besides, Z's suicide can be adequately explained by other reasons.'

'And what are they?'

I paused. Quinn was looking hard at me. I felt a sudden shiver.

'His unsatisfactory home life.'

'I take it, Prentis, you read the statements of Z's colleagues and acquaintances?'

'Yes.'

'They all express unanimous shock at Z's death. No apparent warning signs. No talk of ending it all. No evidence the man was unbalanced. By every account an energetic, successful, well-adjusted man, on top of his job, everything going for him. Then one day he jumps under a Tube train. What do you make of that?'

I hesitated, then tried to sound professional and objective. 'It's a fact, sir, that suicides often appear relaxed and calm before taking their lives – some of the cases we ourselves have handled testify to that. People – '

I hesitated again. Quinn was eyeing me with anticipatory keenness.

'Yes, Prentis?'

'People are known to crack without warning.'

'Indeed, Prentis.' No flicker of the eyelids. 'Sound psychology, I'm sure. But wouldn't a simpler, not to say more likely explanation be that Z's suicide was the result of some quite sudden external factor – for example, a blackmail threat?'

Why was Quinn – the very man who censured it in others – jumping to conclusions?

'In that case, sir, what about the wife's evidence?'

'Oh you mean the wife's *story* . . .' And it was at this point that Quinn's manner became detectably impetuous and excitable. He took his eyes from me for the first time.

'A story, Prentis. Why not? We all know that the best way to hide one guilty secret is seemingly to confess to another. Don't we? Now supposing Z wasn't being blackmailed by X – though X was out to make Z suffer nonetheless. Supposing, as you so rightly suggest, X wasn't a fully-fledged blackmailer; he wasn't after money, he was just a man with a massive chip on his shoulder who simply wanted to get his own back by hurting his betters and concocting groundless slanders. Look at him – an alcoholic, an incompetent, a dead-beat of a man.' Quinn turned his eyes on me again – his face was pink and heated – almost as if he were inviting disagreement. 'Supposing X merely informs Z of something he knows will shatter Z – so shattering, as it turns out, that Z commits suicide. That something relates to Z's wife. The wife is the one with the guilty secret. After her husband's death she herself is in danger of some unpleasant exposure. So, with the perfect cover of the distress of the moment – her grief quite genuine, who knows? – she invents some story about marital havoc, complete with candid and gruesome details. So candid and so intimate that no one dares doubt the truth of it and no one seeks another explanation. Well, isn't it possible? And what do you think of this fellow Z? A perfectly normal man on the evidence of his own colleagues, more than that, successful, a fine career behind – and before him. Treating his wife like that? Attacking his own son? Is it credible?'

Another attack of shivers. If Quinn had worked so long in our office, dealt with the things we dealt with, why was he asking me this? His own phrase: 'lurid imagination'.

'It sounds – if you'll forgive me, sir – a little ... speculative.'

'Speculative! You saw all the evidence in the files.'

'Sir? Which – ?'

'You know about Z's son?'

'Z's son?'

'Yes. Are you telling me you didn't chase that up too? Z's son, Prentis, has been on hostile terms with his mother ever since his father's death. Now why should that be? Think of it, Prentis.' Quinn's voice grew louder. He had got up and was pacing round the room as he spoke, one hand in his pocket, one hand gesturing in the air. 'Think of it. Z was cleared professionally. But all that stuff was dragged out. And suicide. A man with a position and a reputation. You seem in some doubt, Prentis, about the reason for this investigation.' He came right up close to me. 'When your father commits suicide and his name is slurred, isn't that sufficient reason for investigation?'

I felt as the suspect must feel when the hard lights are turned on his eyes. Quinn's face was a mere foot from my own. The flush in his cheeks was matched by the flower in his lapel. Another rose; a small blood-red one.

'I didn't know – '

'It seems to me, Prentis, you don't know quite a lot. Think I'm making this up?'

He bent forwards, both hands in his pockets, like a cross-examining lawyer.

'But if the widow's evidence claimed that Z attacked his own son, it hardly seems – '

'Another of her fabrications – precisely to hide the fact that the son was on the father's side. What's true, Prentis, tell me: what really happens or what people will accept as true?' He began to pace again. 'In any case, even if father and son had once been enemies, it doesn't mean that now – stranger things happen. We know that. Don't we?'

The old bastard.

He turned, moved back towards his desk but did not sit. I watched his limp – a slight drag of the right foot, a lean forward with the shoulder. Crippled body: warped mind? Each of his little probing questions was delivered in an odd, contorted way, as if aimed simultaneously to provoke and deter.

'But – with respect, sir – I don't see why this is an official inquiry. The interests of Z's son aren't an official matter. They don't concern us.'

'Oh you think that, do you? Don't you think that's a rather easy distinction, Prentis – the personal, the official?

We upset people's private lives with our inquiries and then we have the gall to say that private matters don't concern us – not official business. Our investigations caused all the stir, they created the mess – don't you think we should clear it up?'

'I – er – I'm confused.'

'You're confused. You're confused!'

He gave me a merciless look. 'You're confused. You don't know what to think?'

Then a strange thing happened. Standing by his desk, he made a delicate, sweeping, almost magician-like gesture with his hand, as if smoothing out some imaginary rough surface. His face changed, relaxed and put on that old mask of benevolence (or had the mask just been dropped?). I thought: this is madness too. Like the inmates in Dad's hospital: one day they smile and babble affectionately, the next day they glare at you with eyes of steel.

And suddenly I remembered very clearly the face of Mr Forster (hands delving in the bright green cage): a subtle gaze; sly mouth; that strawberry mark above the lip: the face of someone who knows what you don't.

'Well, Prentis.' Quinn pulled back his leather chair. 'Shall we shelve the matter then, you and I? Go no further? Leave well alone? You know what it's like in my job.' He raised both hands, palms upwards. 'You have to carry the can for ordering investigations, for giving information, which might have God knows what consequences.'

I thought: this is it. All this is a fantastic preamble to the subject of my promotion.

He lowered himself into the chair. As he sat down his air of good intention, familiarity increased. He took off his glasses and rubbed his eyes and forehead. A gesture of simple tiredness – or of final, candid concession? Quinn is cracking; he isn't in command at all. He is going to tell everything, confess everything, to treat me ('You and I') as an equal. It may sound odd, but I had the feeling a child has when it knows its parents are happy and everything in the household is harmonious and secure. From along the corridor came the patter of typewriters; the ring of phones; outside, the cherry tree swayed. Quinn rubbed his brow, head lowered, so that I faced the bald, pink part of his scalp. So unprotected. Martin's head under my cricket bat. For the first time I thought of Quinn outside the office, as a private person. At home he would wear cardigans, take in the milk in his dressing-gown. But all this – don't think I had entirely lost my guard – was tempered by the fear that at any moment he might say something to make that icy feeling return. An idea was forming in my mind that I was half afraid Quinn could somehow see. The strange pertinency of his questions, and the C9 case. What did he know about me? About Dad, Marian and the boys. All this talk of investigation. Supposing Quinn were investigating me?

He raised his head, replaced his glasses and spread his hands on the desk. Now –

But he did not speak of my promotion. Every line in my face must have shown him that I was hoping he would do so.

'So we drop it then? Let it lie?'

He pushed his head forward and peered hard at me. Grey-blue, alert eyes, like Martin's. What did he want me to say? The eyes flickered, behind the lenses of his glasses, as if some crucial issue rested on my answer; as if some conflict in Quinn's own conscience hung upon it.

I gave the coward's response.

'I really don't know, sir. Is this such a special case?'

'Every one of our cases is special for someone, Prentis.'

He looked me up and down. An officer assessing some picked man.

'To get back to my original point, Prentis. About the past histories of X and Z – and Z's son, if it comes to it. I take it that you did *look* at what there was on that?'

'I'm afraid – there wasn't anything, sir.'

'Wasn't anything? But you looked at file E?'

'File E, sir?'

'File E.'

I tried to meet his eyes. 'File E wasn't on the shelves, sir.'

'Oh, not on the shelves? Is that so? Is that so, Prentis?'

There was a long pause – long enough for a challenge, or an explanation. And suddenly the mask – the face – was gone.

'Right, that will be all, Prentis.'

He picked up a pile of papers on his desk, shuffled them, put them to one side, picked up another pile and, with the air of some tireless robot, began working through them, as if I were no longer in the room.

'Well, what are you waiting for, man?'

I must act soon.

14

It is almost the end of May. The weather is getting hotter.
In the Tube at rush-hours people are getting restless. I can
tell by their quick eyes, by the way they barely tolerate
each other's sticky, jostling bodies, each other's need to
occupy space of their own. Something must happen soon.
All this packing together of nature into unnatural circumstances must lead to something.

Two or three times, when I've emerged at Clapham
South onto the pavement, I've had this urge to take off my
tie, my socks and shoes – to go no further – and simply to
walk away; as if Clapham Common were some endless,
enveloping savannah. But, of course, I don't. I turn to my
left, along Nightingale Lane, and shamble home, like any
man returning from work, clad in his weariness, his per-
plexities, his frustrations. If you were to pass me by, it would
not surprise me if you noticed my brows contract tightly
every so often (I have inherited from Dad that intermittent
little knot of lines above the nose and between the eyebrows,
though in my case it makes me look simply harassed, not
nobly thoughtful) and my lips move and mutter indistinct,
garbled words. They say if you want to see a man as he

really is, catch him unawares, when he isn't thinking of being seen. Well, that's the time to catch me. When I'm not under the eye of Quinn or of my family – and I'm free from the scrutiny of the Tube. That's when I am what I am, I don't deny it. But recently I've been keeping a check on myself, even during these permissive moments. I've been developing an eager, erect carriage as I step homeward, a brisk, confident pace (in this heat) and imitating the zeal of some of my fellow commuters. For not all of them drift home like zombies capable of walking under a bus without noticing it. Some of them launch themselves from the station with an energy unsapped by the rigours of the day, shirt collars seemingly undirtied, briefcases and papers jauntily gripped, and sail buoyantly along the pavement, eager to embrace wives, dandle children and nurture gardens; and whether they are acting or not I don't know. But I've been induced to ape them in a quite fraudulent manner myself.

That evening – after I'd seen Quinn about C9 – as I came up out of the Tube, I had the distinct sensation of being watched. I don't know whose eyes I expected to see – suddenly averted when they met my own, peering maybe from a parked car or from behind some screening newspaper – or whether I felt less under the gaze of particular eyes than of some nebulous presence. I brushed the feeling aside. But it suddenly struck me later, when I was half way home and I had lapsed into my usual distracted manner: what if someone with an interest in me were really to see me, slouching home like this, my expression vexed and brooding, mumbling inanely to myself? That would hardly bear investigation. If someone had their spies ... I had been thinking – so absorbedly that I was scarcely conscious of my route along the pavement – of that afternoon's bizarre interview, of C9, of what Quinn would do next, what I should do; and then suddenly, as if, had I looked behind me, Quinn himself or Quinn's agent would have been there, I automatically straightened my shoulders, smartened my pace and put on an alert, ebullient expression. I had to look normal, cheerful and undaunted, not to betray my confusion, my suspicion. Even when it least seemed I could be under inspection.

And it was just then, as I walked along the edge of the common that I really did discover someone watching me. It was not Quinn. It was Martin. He was standing some thirty or forty yards away, out on the common, and such was his attitude when I saw him that I somehow knew we hadn't just spotted each other by accident: he had been following me at a distance, stalking me, perhaps all the way from the station. I stepped onto the grass, raised my hand, and was about to shout 'Martin!' when he turned abruptly and began walking off in another direction, as if pretending he hadn't seen me or I had made some mistake. But I knew it was Martin. He was wearing Martin's yellow T-shirt and jeans. I don't believe in mirages on Clapham Common.

What was he doing? I readily admit that I have this recurring hope (which is not such a far-fetched and fantastic hope, after all) that one day my sons will come to meet me at the station. That seems the sort of gesture that children who care for their fathers are glad to make. And, believe me, I'd be chuffed to bits if they did. But Martin hadn't come to meet me. If he had he would have been waiting by the newsagent's or the florist's. He had come to observe his father, as one observes some creature under glass, at just that time of day when I am most, so to speak, in my natural state. And it struck me – even as I stood with my hand half-raised and my mouth open as he walked away – that he must have witnessed enough to label me as a pretty sickly specimen; a shuffling, half-crazed figure; a figure who scarcely merited his esteem – if that had not already been established by the episode of Dad's book. And not only this, but he must have seen, just before I spotted him, that sudden change come over me as if I were putting on a disguise and pretending to be a different man. Would he have interpreted this as the seal upon my patent hypocrisy – a little process I went through every evening in order to present myself to my family? Or as a guilty reaction (nearer the immediate truth) to the fear of being observed? Either way, a complete sham. I stood at the edge of the grass watching Martin's yellow back slipping into the shadows of the chestnuts. I thought of calling him again, but I didn't. And why had he walked away like that? As a deliberate display of spurning me? Or as some subtle indication of our relations? Shadowing me all the way from the station, like some Indian brave watching the pale-face pass along the trail, and then turning at the moment of being, perhaps quite calculatedly, glimpsed, as if it were for me to settle the question of our future hostility or friendship. I remembered the feeling I had had that morning Martin gave back Dad's book, that I must make amends to him, not he to me; that I was the one to seek forgiveness, not he. I lost Martin's yellow T-shirt. All around – I had scarcely noticed them up to now – people were relaxing in the evening sun, playing games or lounging on the grass, like inmates in some institution allowed time for recreation.

Almost the first thing I said when I got in was: 'Where's Martin?'

'He went out.'

'Where?'

'He just said "out".'

Marian was washing lettuce for a salad and she said nothing more and scarcely looked up. I have noticed she is getting like this of late. Quieter, shrinking, far-off. More and more thrifty with her words, as she is becoming, in bed, more and more thrifty with her body.

'You mean you just let him wander off and you haven't a clue where he's going?'

Peter came down the stairs from his bedroom. I am still trying to work out whether he was in on the business of Dad's book. He has a way now, when I get in from work, of coming dutifully to the front door and saying mechanically, 'Hello, Dad.' But there is this anxious, timid look in his face which, until very recently, both pleased me and puzzled me. I've arrived at the explanation now. It's not that he's in awe of me. Not at all. But he's in awe of his brother. Whether he was an accomplice to it or not, he's impressed by Martin's daring, and for the first time in his little life he is feeling the onus of something to live up to. He wonders if he could do what Martin did, if he could be so bold. It's a strange thing how your own kids suddenly start to reveal to you the implicit shape of their lives. If Martin will take after his grandfather, Peter will take after me. Poor mite. Already, in these few weeks, Martin's face seems to have become firmly moulded; Peter's is soft and elusive.

'Hello, Peter. Know where Martin is?'

His eyes sharpen. Of course, all my theories could be wrong.

Then I said, to both of them: 'Well, didn't he say when he'd be back?'

They looked at me without speaking, as if they had detected some tell-tale symptom in my behaviour.

Then it almost seemed that a cloud passed over my eyes. Supposing they're all in it, all together? Quinn and Martin and Marian and Peter?

15

There is nothing to stop me making inquiries of my own. In fact there is every facility to assist me. I have only to procure the standard forms and covering letters from the office and send them to the right addresses. Such requests for information, of course, should really be authorized and signed by Quinn, but it is ten-to-one in my favour that, given the obtuseness of bureaucracy, they will be taken in by the official documents and not query my own signature. I know where the forms are kept. How many times have I filled up at Quinn's behest these formidable sheets of paper headed sternly 'STRICTLY CONFIDENTIAL'? In fact, only now does it strike me – perhaps I am a naïve and simple-minded creature, after all – what opportunities exist for such as I for delving into untold privacies, for obtaining almost unlimited access into the darker byways of other people's lives. All I have to do is to pick out the forms, draft my request – 'Details of the personal histories of X and Z prior to their employment in H.M. service' – have it typed – not by Quinn's secretary, I will ask Maureen, who won't be aware of what she is doing – and have it franked and despatched. The only risk is if Quinn or any of my colleagues catches me at it. I will have to choose some time when the office is quiet. Not at night, after normal hours. Quinn will be working late too. That is the one time when I will look most suspicious. At lunch-time perhaps. Or, better still, early in the morning. Quinn himself rarely appears before half past nine, and I can invent some pretext for the office messengers to let me in before eight. I can have everything done by nine and then take it through to the typing pool with a batch of routine items later in the day.

And if my correspondents at the Home Office don't fail me, if they don't hesitate to give information they must already have imparted once, then I shall have it both ways. I shall know, a little at least, of what is in File E, without having to challenge Quinn for it. And if I discover something he is trying to hide – then, I shall be able to challenge him.

16

'Martin wants to know' (it's two days later, a Thursday: Marian and I are in bed) 'why you went to work at a different time today.'

'Oh? What's that to him?'

'You had breakfast by yourself and went in early, and then you were home about five.'

'I know.'

'Martin thinks you're avoiding him.'

So – he was waiting again for me on the common – but I was early.

'Look, has Martin said anything about coming to meet me at the station?'

'No. Why?'

'Nothing. I thought I saw him a couple of times, coming home.'

'You flatter yourself. Coming to meet *you* at the station.'

Marian is lying with her back towards me. Her voice comes to me as if from behind a wall.

'I don't see why he shouldn't from time to time.'

'Come to think of it, why *did* you go into work early?'

Marian turns to face me. As she turns, her small breasts turn with her, like another pair of fleshy eyes. We are naked – just for the heat. We haven't made love for some time now. We seem to have put away our sexual play-kit.

'I had some extra work to do. I've gone in early before, haven't I?'

'But you've always told me. I didn't know you weren't going to have breakfast.'

Marian's eyes suddenly become limpid and soulful (is that such a dreadful thing – missing breakfast?).

'You don't tell me anything these days.'

I thought: Now is the time I could tell her. Marian, I am going to be promoted.

'It was only for today. I'll go in at the usual time tomorrow.'

'You might have told me.' She frowns. 'What was this extra work anyway?'

'Look – enough of all these questions.' My voice goes up a pitch. For a moment there's almost a danger of it cracking guiltily. Why should she ask that?

'Sorry. I only thought – '

She bites her lip. Her eyes are still wide and dreamily fixed on me, but as she looks it is as though she is drifting away. Some anaesthetic is clouding her vision and she can no longer recognize me. I think of Martin turning his back, on the common.

I move towards her and put my hand over her navel. She sighs audibly and goes passive and limp, though, in a way, this is just the same as her body going hard and impenetrable. I run my hand over her as if over some unfamiliar object. Things will go no further; but then I'm not moved by desire so much as by some sense of dreadful loneliness. My wife is afraid of me, she does not know me. I draw closer and put my mouth to her breast (unresisting, unprotected) and very gently peck her nipples.

'It was only for today. You can tell Martin that if you like . . . Marian?'

And sure enough, I saw him, tonight (Friday), under the trees, the other side of the bowling green, as I passed. What does he want? All right, so he has seen me, that first time, for what I really am. And he knows that this figure who walks manfully by, for his benefit, and the benefit of who knows what other hidden observers, is no more than a puppet. And he knows that I know he knows that. What more does he want? All right, so he is nearly eleven years old and finding his strength, and I am three times his age and wondering where I mislaid mine; hoping to be propped up by some promotion. All right, I am the one to blame. Does he want me to confess as much to his face? To get down on my knees?

Tonight I stepped off the pavement and walked towards him over the grass. He had already turned and moved off as he saw me change course. He quickened his pace, intuitively, without looking back, as I quickened mine. This was like one of those dreams in which you try to reach the ones you love but you can't. They'd cut the grass on that part of the common, and hanging in the air was the sweet, sappy smell that makes you know it's summer. 'Martin!' I called. And I wanted to add: 'Don't go. Please. I'm sorry.' Then, when my longer stride began to tell on him, he broke into a run. He ran towards the zebra-crossing on the South Circular Road. The South Circular Road divides one part of the common from the other; on the far side is the duck pond. I remembered the time when the boys were younger but just old enough to go out by themselves, and we lived in dread of their little bodies being smashed by cars. I started to run too but stopped almost at once, suddenly aware of appearing foolish. I wasn't going to go chasing after my own son.

17

Subject: Z, Arthur Leonard.

Born, June 12th, 1921; Hemfield, Nr East Grinstead, Sussex. Only son of Hon. Sir Geoffrey Robert, D.S.O., M.B.E., formerly Captain, Royal Hampshire Regt (born, Jan. 25th, 1894) and Katherine Elizabeth (née Phillips, born, Oct. 2nd, 1897).

Educ.: Oakwood Preparatory School, East Grinstead; Tonbridge School; Wadham College, Oxford (Law: 1937/8).

University career curtailed by outbreak of war. Joined R.A.F., 1940. Trained as fighter-pilot. Sqdns 80, 225; N. Africa, 1941–2. Grounded after accident in training exercise in which one flying officer killed and subject injured. R.A.F. Intelligence, London, 1942–5. 2 applications for retraining as pilot refused. Air Ministry, 1945–6.

Left R.A.F., 1946. Did not resume law studies (apparent cause of family dissension). Applied unsuccessfully, Foreign Office (subject spoke good French), 1947. Entered Home Office, 1947. Subsequent career of distinction. Married Yvette Simone (née Debreuil, born, May 10th, 1922; family from Chambéry, France) July,

1947. Resident at 19, Clifford Terrace, Kensington till 1950, then at 8, Peele Gardens, Putney (till suicide of subject).

Sir Geoffrey appointed K.C. 1938. Assisted at Nuremberg War Trials, 1945–6. Judge of the High Court of Justice, 1948. Chaired/Adv. Cttees. of Inquiry (Legal Rights of Prisoners; Aspects of International Law) 1959, 1960–61, 1962–3. Retired, 1964. Published: *Sword and Pen* (memoirs of military and legal career), 1965; *Reasonable Doubt* (critique of English jurisprudence), 1967.

Katherine Elizabeth victim of long and complicated illness from 1964. Operations for cancer. Died 1967.

Sir Geoffrey died 1968.

Richard Geoffrey, son of subject, born, July 22nd, 1949. Educ: Westminster School, London School of Economics. Present occupation, journalist.

Elaine Elizabeth, daughter of subject, born, March 14th, 1951. Educ.: The Lodge High School, Putney; Camberwell School of Art. Formed liaison with Karl Lageröf, Swedish commercial artist, 1970. At present resident in Stockholm.

Only the details on Z so far. The information on X 'in preparation and to follow'. Impossible, therefore, to look for connexions. So why do I linger over these potted facts? Is it because I have obtained them by my own initiative and ingenuity, proved how easy it is for one person, with neither the right nor the authority, to secure for himself the private history of another? Or is it that there is really something arresting, something appealing about these bare bones of a life (how many such skeletons have I cursorily pieced together at the department?) when it is you yourself who have scooped them up with your net? Those little tokens of dignity and esteem. The father's military and civil honours. '*Sword and Pen*'. 'Career of distinction'. Z cursed by an accident. The daughter running off with a Swede. 'Family dissension'. Those place-names of imperturbable gentility: East Grinstead, Tonbridge, Peele Gardens, Putney. Suicide; war-crimes; 'long and complicated illness'.

Or does something particular strike a chord? Debreuil? Wasn't that the name of the firm of engineers with which Dad worked before the war, building embankments on the Rhône and road tunnels in the Savoy Alps – and where he learnt the fluent French he would put to use in the years to come? And Z's Christian name: Arthur, Arthur . . . Why does that suddenly have an echo?

It is gone midnight. Marian is in bed. I sit in the living-room looking at these notes which I have smuggled home with me against all the rules, not even daring to look at them in the office. The window is open, an occasional breeze lifts the papers in front of me; and I remember Dad, sitting up late at Wimbledon, working on his book. Mother asleep in the big bedroom. Getting up once, in summer, to fetch a glass of water; pausing at the half-opened door, the desk lamp on inside, and seeing him suddenly start.

And now, when I turn to the other sheet – 'Details of Subject's Private Connexions outside the Home Office' – which I have also requested, some last incidental entry makes the echo come loud and clear.

. . . Hon. Sec, The Putney Rotary.
Clubs: Oxford and Cambridge; Civil Service.
Sports and Recreations: Golf. The Glade Golf Club, Wimbledon.

18

It is to the last two chapters of *Shuttlecock* that I return most frequently. It is not just that, even to the casual and disinterested reader, they must form the most exciting, the most dramatic pages of the book: Dad's capture by the Gestapo; his imprisonment for eight days in the Château Martine, the Gestapo headquarters near the village of Combe-les-Dames; his escape; his flight through the forests of the Doubs valley; his awaking after a desperate night in hiding to discover, through the trees, not Germans, but advancing Americans, and his declaring himself (last, succinct scene of the book) to a Seventh Army lieutenant ('a lawyer's son from Connecticut, with impeccable politeness and a truck-load of canned meat'). No, it is not this air of grand denouement alone which compels me, but other qualities, more subtle, more tantalizing . . .

For one thing, there are the gaps, the hazy areas in those eight days at the Château Martine. The Château is there all right, starting from the pages, its eighteenth-century elegance given over to twentieth-century brutality: the pitch-dark cells; the ornate staircases and passage-ways (on the way to interrogation sessions); the degrading musters in the courtyard; the smells, the rifleshots, the food ('unspeakable swill'); the cries along corridors. Even the Château garden is there, for contrast ('as unreal as some painting by Watteau or Claude'), glimpsed, again, through tall, casement windows, on those journeys to the interrogation room. But it is about the goings-on in that interrogation room, and other, sinister rooms, that Dad is silent, or circumspect. The picture clouds over: a few vague allusions, a hint of the inarticulable ('Here description must be blurred'), a few chilly motifs.

All right, there are obvious reasons for this. The stress of circumstances which tested even Dad's presence of mind, tenacity and powers of observation; which ten years later, late at night, in a room in Wimbledon, left gaping holes in the memory. Or the reverse? The memory not in the least impaired, still vivid-sharp; but the memory of something so terrible that it cannot be repeated, cannot be spoken or written of.

Did they torture you, Dad? Did they stretch you to the limit? And yet you write of things terrible enough – things which occurred only days before they dragged you out of that water tank and hauled you off to the Château – with relative composure.

... For with the German retreat through the eastern valleys the war entered a quite new, if, thankfully, brief-lived phase. Up to then we had lived in a world, superficially at least, at peace, disturbed and broken intermittently by incidents of violence, often savage it is true, but localized and in the majority of cases directly influenced by ourselves. With the waves of German troops, the tide of indiscriminate large-scale war, which had not been known for years, rolled into this corner of France. Not merely war on a large scale but war with all the desperation and last-reserve venom of an army in defeat. This was a period of burning villages, of corpses lining the streets and dangling from trees, of atrocities of all kinds. Whole areas of countryside which up till this time had seemed for us inviolable and friendly landmarks suddenly became ravaged, contaminated. Everywhere was the smell of blood, carnage, singed and rotting flesh . . .

I have been trying to discover in these and other pages some clue to what happened in the Château Martine, some inkling of this experience beyond words. My own father tortured. Forced, perhaps, beyond the point of endurance. Why do I want to know this – like some interrogator myself ? Because I will find out what Dad is really like?

But there is something else that draws me back to these last two chapters. Something harder to explain. These pages are more vivid, more real, more believable than any other part of the book. And yet, strangely enough, this is because the style of Dad's writing becomes – how shall I put it? – more imaginative, more literary, more speculative. In the main body of the book – so I've explained – only the occasional brief passage of reflection, of emotion, breaks the brisk, adventure-book flow of the narrative. But in these final chapters it is as though the philosophic note is always there (that theme of war-in-peace and peace-in-war, for instance); and Dad's words seem ever ready to take on a quieter, sadder, even eloquent tone – not at all the tone of the man who, quickly sizing the situation, stuck the knife into the guard's back at Caen. It is there even in the description of those destructive retreating armies:

. . . All day long the columns poured through Dôle and Auxonne and on in the direction of Besançon and Vesoul. They left behind a wake of devastation. And yet it was impossible not to feel a degree of pity for these streams of weary, ill-kempt men who were no longer heroes or conquerors, ill-equipped and ill-transported, moving on, fleeing, like migrating animals obeying a mass instinct, up the river valleys, towards Mulhouse, the Rhine, and home . . .

It is there in the very lines which follow those about the 'contamination' of the landscape:

. . . I remember there was a wood, a mile or so outside Ligny, a small wood of no great distinction – oaks, sweet chestnuts and hazels – but in which pheasants cackled and the sun fell on drifts of dead leaves. We must have skirted it, on bicycle or on foot, several hundred times, and unconsciously come to regard it as an emblem of things that would continue unchanged, regardless of the war. One day a group of five Maquisards were pinned down in this wood, and the Germans, in order to make sure of despatching them, poured mortar shell after mortar shell into it. I passed it soon afterwards: a smouldering, twisted array of stumps. Two of the five men I had known – and that week was to bring worse human tragedies; but I felt the loss of that wood like few human losses. The thing that most embodies the evil of war, is not, it seems to me, its human violence (for humans cause wars), but its wilful disregard for nature . . .

And it is there on the penultimate page, before that awakening in the forest and the polite lieutenant from Connecticut:

. . . I made a hollow in the undergrowth, covering myself with leaves, and curled up in it. Some tall beech trees groaned in the wind above me. I was shivering, semi-delirious, hungry, had lost my sense of direction and did not know where I was. I remember thinking, before drifting into merciful sleep, Yes, I am no better than some burrowing animal . . .

19

Another Wednesday. The evenings are getting longer. Under the cedar tree, on the bench, in the hospital grounds, I had this feeling of calm, of refuge. I was safe here. As the sun sets, the red bricks of the hospital walls start to glow; the windows gleam like copper. You do not have to put yourself at risk at all or endanger anything if you never make a move.

For a long time I sat beside Dad, as silent and as still as he was, and I thought: this could go on for ever. Sometimes I wonder what I am more afraid of: of Dad never breaking his silence, or of his suddenly speaking.

I don't know why this weight lay on my tongue, which only a while before, on my drive down, had been itching with questions. It is easy to frame questions when you know there will be no answers. I wanted to say to him: what does the name Debreuil mean to you? Tell me about Z. Tell me. Yet what I wanted to ask, even more than this, was: What happened, Dad, in the Château Martine? Did they torture you? But I didn't. I sat in silence several minutes more. It seemed to me we were like two weights on a balance, a swaying see-saw, precariously poised. And then I said:

'I have got some news, Dad. I am going to be promoted. Quinn told me. Have I told you about my boss Quinn?'

Sometimes Dad is so still and sits so rigidly, it seems that if I touched him with the tip of my finger and gave just a slight push, he would topple, slowly and ponderously, onto the grass.

When I left the hospital the calm feeling still hung around me, though it slowly wore off, so that as I drove through Sutton and Morden I started to look in the driving mirror to see if I was being followed (a new habit), and my tongue started to itch again to ask those questions I had meant to ask Dad. As I neared home it was itching even more, though not to ask questions – to shout at Marian and the kids.

You know those surprisingly long, light evenings in early summer, when lilacs bloom in gardens and even in such mundane and humdrum places as Sutton and Morden a breath of peace seems to hang in the air as if it were really hanging over some wide, virgin landscape. On the way home I took a detour towards Wimbledon. I drove up to the golf course and pulled up in the car-park by the club-house. It was the sort of lingering end to the day (long shadows, a faint breeze, a sweet scent to the turf) which golfers must love. The light was beginning to fade but I could see several figures still, in coloured sweaters and flapping trousers, out on the fairways. The lights were on in the club-house and the doors open. I could hear a babble of voices. Someone was talking loudly about the price of property. The car-park had been enlarged and an extension added to the club-house since the days I remembered. Several members were already leaving to go home, jingling car-keys with a satisfied air and shouting sarcasms to friends across the gravel. It didn't seem that their plummy, somewhat hollow voices were the equivalent of the voices I had heard when I was a boy, but perhaps they were.

I went into the club-house. There were men with reddened faces and cigars sitting at the bar. They looked at me suspiciously. The barman looked at me suspiciously too. Against one of the walls was a glass-fronted cabinet containing silver cups and plates and, fixed to the wall, polished wooden boards recording the winners of annual tournaments and competitions. The names went back over thirty years. Amongst them, appearing in one instance ('55–'57), three times in succession, was Dad's name. But there was no name with the initials A. L. Not a winner, I thought. I could say to the men with cigars, like some hard-talking detective, Which ones of you knew Prentis? Did anyone here know Z? (Why is it that the questions fail you when you most think they will lead somewhere?) The barman was still looking at me curiously. I said: 'It's all right, I'm looking for someone – not here,' and turned to the door.

I loitered a little while at the edge of the car-park. Golf courses, like commons, try to marry wildness with civility. Dusk was falling. The sweatered figures were trailing in across the grass, like returning hunters, with their trolleys and bags. As the light faded the clumps of birches and hawthorns seemed to loom more definitely, and then only the little fluorescent marker-flags stood out, like sentinels, on the greens.

It kept ringing in my mind, as if, were I to turn round, they would all be standing there: 'Arthur, Arthur.'

The figures drew near and I could hear their breathy, invigorated voices.

Wwwhack! Wwwhack!

20

Today Quinn said to me, 'Hear you've been coming into work early, Prentis. That's commendably diligent of you.' A tiny, ironically indulgent smile. But his eyes gave a little rigid stare, as if to show he knew everything and was gloating in his knowledge; as if, even with one of those podgy, pink hands of his, he could pick me up, tie me in knots, crush me. He had come down for once from his eyrie, down his flight of steps, and was favouring us with a visit. He was going round, this little plump man, amongst his juniors, who are all bigger and stronger than he, and yet they were saying, as he handed out routine instructions, 'Thank you sir. Yes sir.'

'By the way, any more thoughts on C9?'

Today he wore a white carnation.

And tonight Marian said, 'It's not like you to bring home work from the office. What's going on?'

All this week – in spite of what I promised Marian – I have been going in early to secure any mail addressed to me, and then at night, at home, staying up late, going over those details on Z, pondering and making notes, so that when I've at last gone to bed Marian has been asleep. We hardly exchange words. But tonight she was awake, her eyes peering at me over the covers. When I shrugged off her question and said, clambering into bed, 'A special job I have to do,' she looked hard and searchingly at me for a while, then twisted round and hunched up like something going into its shell. She lies with her knees drawn up, her body curled and her chin lowered into her throat so that, even though the weather is hot, she looks like someone huddling for warmth and protection.

Marian, I wish I knew.

21

Martin is still following me from the station. Despite the change in my time of returning from work. Every evening but one I have glimpsed his shock of fair hair amongst the trees on the common, and every evening when we sit together at supper, we pretend not to have seen each other. I don't know what to do. It is his birthday in two weeks. He will be eleven. I am thinking of buying him a pet.

22

... Subject: X, Ronald Francis. Home Office, 1950–73. Dismissed: gross misconduct and on medical grounds (alcoholism).

Born, Highgate, London, March 2nd, 1920. Son of William Rycroft ...

And, after a catalogue of unremarkable data concerning family background, upbringing and education:

... Studied (Modern French Literature), Sorbonne, Paris, 1937–9. 1940–44, Officer, Royal Fusiliers. Served, North Africa, Sicily. Attached Special Operations, March 1944. Operating British agent, France (Franche-Comté), June–Oct. 1944. Prisoner of SS (Doubs), Sept. 1944. Liberated by Americans ...

23

Today I did it. I went to see Quinn. To have it out with him. I said: 'Sir, I want to know what's going on.'

Now it's true I rarely go to see Quinn without his first summoning me. And yet today, when I had taken the initiative myself, when I had asked over the office intercom (what daring!) for permission to see him as soon as possible – 'about a special matter' – and he had replied, 'Very well, in ten minutes,' he was not in the least taken aback. When he buzzed for me and I entered, the work on his desk was pushed to one side, he was sitting with his hands clasped neatly before him (carnation in buttonhole), as if in some way he had long prepared for this visit of mine (perhaps, after all, it really was *he* who summoned me). As if he knew this was a big moment.

'Well, Prentis, what can I do for you?'

Naturally, all this readiness threw me off my guard. I sat down at his bidding. I had rehearsed my opening in advance. It spilled out like some self-conscious statement made in court:

'Sir, I must speak to you about something that's been on my mind – concerning the department – for some time. What I have to say, if you'll permit me, is merely a considered observation – nothing more – which I feel obliged to make by my position here in the office. It's quite possible that I may be intruding into matters which shouldn't concern me and which have a perfectly satisfactory official explanation. In which case, sir, I'd be grateful – I'd quite understand – if you'll tell me when I'm venturing too far.'

Even as I spoke I thought: What studied, what ingratiating servility. Out with it! Accuse him face to face: You've been stealing office files.

'Good heavens, Prentis, what an introduction. You'd better go on.'

The eyes expressed curiosity, but not alarm.

I thought: It's not too late to change tack; to avoid wrecking my promotion prospects; to avoid Quinn's wrath. I could hastily invent some other story which wouldn't launch me into trouble.

He looked at me as I paused. But, strangely enough, it wasn't fear of Quinn which made me hesitate at this point. Somehow I knew I could bear his worst retribution. It was a recurrence of the opposite thing, the thing I had experienced before. What if in the face of my veiled accusations this inscrutable, imperious man should crumble? What if the consequence of my words should be to expose him, to jeopardize his own long and almost completed career, and that I should sit in power over him. Would I be able to bear that?

'Sir, I can't help having noticed – for some months now – that certain files in this office have been missing from their normal places. Not having had the use of these files has hampered work on a number of cases I've handled

– which, if I may say so, have at the same time, even in terms of the available data, been disjointed and confusing. I know that documents and whole files can, in the normal course of things, be removed for reference – er – at a level higher than my own. But such items are usually returned after a short period and, in any case, a proper record is kept of their use. The files I am speaking of, sir – I believe' (don't cringe!) 'I have alluded to them in conversations with you before – have never returned. If you wish, sir – I had made a list – '

Nothing ruffled the plump face. A mistake! A catastrophic error of judgement! The eyes looked straight at me. He put a hand to one cheek, propping his elbow on the armrest of his leather chair, and gently rubbed his mouth with the knuckle of his little finger.

'Let me get this clear, Prentis. What you are saying now isn't just some passing misunderstanding. Is that right? What you are voicing is a strong, long-harboured suspicion?'

'I – '

'Well, is it?'

'Yes sir.'

'I see. And what would you say if I were to say to you that this suspicion of yours is none of your business?'

'I – er – would have to accept your word on the matter, sir.'

'Yes, yes. But would it stop your suspicion?'

'No sir.'

'Would it in fact prevent you from taking steps of your own to follow up your suspicion?'

'I – er – No sir.'

'In other words, you think that something in this office

demands investigation and if necessary you yourself, on your own initiative, would carry out that investigation?'

But now he didn't allow me time to answer.

'Ironic, Prentis, isn't it? We are the ones who investigate others. That we should have to investigate ourselves.'

He smiled sourly. It was the first hint of some possible confession. I felt afraid.

'Tell me, Prentis. Missing files, mixed-up files ... Been going on for some months you say. So what's kept you quiet up to now? Is there something else, perhaps, you haven't yet mentioned?'

The eyes sharpened, as if my thoughts were on view.

'Perhaps, sir ... But I'd rather clear up the general issue first.'

'You'd rather clear up the general issue first. Hmmh. You see, if I were a suspicious man – like you, Prentis – and if, let's suppose for the sake of argument, something really is "going on" – I might be saying to myself now that what you call this "considered observation" isn't really a considered observation at all but some sort of disguised allegation. And I'd be saying to myself that a man like Prentis wouldn't just come out with an allegation by itself like that. He'd back it up with a little bit of homework of his own. I've been watching you, Prentis. You're suspicious, all right, and crafty – and' (his face seemed to draw suddenly closer) 'just a little bit desperate. So – I'd better find out what information he's got up his sleeve before either I make some stupid denial or incriminate myself. It's lucky for you, Prentis, I'm not a suspicious man.'

'Sir, I – '

'No, no, it's all right. You're a responsible junior, acting according to his conscience.'

He took off his glasses and began to rub them diligently with a handkerchief. When people take off their glasses it gives them a vulnerable appearance; but at this moment it was as though Quinn was indicating he was prepared to fight without artificial protection.

'You know I'll be leaving this job in three and a half months.'

'Yes sir.'

'It won't be me who's sitting here then. Three and a half months.'

He held up his glasses to the light, squinted at them, huffed, and began rubbing again.

'Tell me something else, Prentis. Allow me to ask some questions just for the moment. You'll have your turn for yours to be answered, but let me clear up mine first. The others – Fletcher, Clarke, O'Brien – have they noticed any of these things you've mentioned?'

'I don't know, sir. They may have done, but never spoken about it.'

'But nonetheless, it's you and not one of them who's come forward with this suspicion. Why do you think that is?'

'I don't know, sir. I am – the most senior of them. And – with respect sir – there have been previous occasions, talking with you – '

'Could it just be that they are simple, trusting souls who want a quiet life and ask no questions?'

He finished polishing his glasses and replaced them over his nose.

'How long have you been in this department, Prentis?'

'Eight years.'

'Do you think it's a good job?'

'I can't complain, sir.' (Liar. You're a persecuted little drudge.) 'The conditions, the—'

'No, no, no. I mean the function we perform here. Do you think it's a good one?'

'I don't know it's something you can judge like that. Basically, we provide information.'

'But do you think it's a good thing to provide information?'

He got up and moved towards the window, turning his back towards me.

'Have you had moments in your life, Prentis, when you've found yourself asking the simple question: Is it better to know things or not to know them? Wouldn't we sometimes be happier not knowing them? Know what I mean?'

For a moment I thought: He's stalling. He's not going to tell me anything. I will have to resort to other methods. Break into his office at night and crack his safe. Silence the security guard with a stiletto . . .

'I think so, sir.'

'And what's your answer been?'

'I don't know. Circumstances usually decide that for you. It can be – a torment *not* knowing things.'

'Ah yes. Quite so. You suffer either way.'

He turned round, away from the window. For some reason his face seemed pinker and pudgier than I'd ever known it.

'Do you know what I think of this job, Prentis?'

'No sir.'

'It's – uncomfortable. That chair – ' he pointed to the big black leather chair which, though unoccupied, seemed to have a masterful, sinister quality of its own –

'is uncomfortable. Try it. All this information we sit on, Prentis. Do you know how I sometimes imagine this place? A big cupboard for the collected skeletons of half the metropolitan population. And I'm the one with the key. Oh, I don't mean the things we have to let out for quite specific reasons. But just think for a moment of all those innocent, unwitting people whose peace of mind might be shattered by some little titbit we have here. It's an odd thing, Prentis, looking at other people's lives and seeing the dangers that they're unaware of. Like – looking at a fly and wondering: shall I swot it?'

As it happened – as though expressly to provide Quinn with his image – a fly had flown into the room through the opened window only minutes before, and after buzzing several times round the desk settled on the rim of a cup of coffee which Quinn had only half drunk. Yet, oddly enough, he did not brush it away.

'There was a time when I didn't like this job, Prentis. All this accumulated evil, constantly sifting through it. You have to admit it gets you down. It sticks to your hands, so to speak. Doesn't it?'

'Er, yes sir.'

'I used to tell myself that the solution was simply to curb one's imagination. You've heard me tell you to do just that enough times, haven't you? But you can no more curb the imagination than you can stop the truth being what it is. Do you follow me, Prentis?'

'I'm not sure, sir.'

'Never mind. Then I started to think that precisely because I had access to all this evil, I was in a position to do real good. I thought, perhaps one can wipe out certain harms simply by erasing the record of those harms. With me? But I'm not sure, now, if you can do that. I'm not sure at all.'

He moved across the room and perched himself on the edge of his desk. There was something almost comical about this casual posture in a man like Quinn. His lame leg swung and knocked against the panelling of the desk with an oddly solid thump.

'What do you think, Prentis? Is it right?'

Once more, he did not wait for my reply. He twisted round and pressed the intercom on his desk.

'Miss Reynolds – be a dear and bring in another *two* cups of coffee.'

He turned back and took a deep breath. 'I seem to have said enough, don't I? No, I'm not trying to duck your questions. I'll answer them. But I don't know if this is the right time or place.' He picked up a diary from the desk. 'You want to know – everything, don't you? Would you care to come and see me, one evening after work – at my home?'

Two years ago, if Quinn had invited me to his home, I would have gone, uneasily, regarding it as an office duty. Now I was not sure whether I was walking into some strange friendship – or a trap.

'You look alarmed, Prentis. Yes, I know. Nobody knows much about me outside the office. The office persona and all that.' He smiled sourly again. 'You probably know more about any number of people in our records than you do about me. But I do have a home, and a home life of sorts.'

He had a pen poised over the diary.

'What day would you like? You can get to Richmond?'

'Richmond?'

'Richmond, yes.'

'Wednesday?' I don't know why I said that day.

'Wednesday. Fine. Shall we say about eight? Ah – Miss Reynolds.'

Miss Reynolds (a frosty-faced spinster of some years, renowned in the office as 'The Iron Lady', and the perfect partner to Quinn) entered with a tray with coffee and biscuits. She put it down on Quinn's desk and removed the dirty cup – from which the fly buzzed upwards. She brushed at it with her hand, then left the room.

Quinn, like the avuncular figure in the biscuit commercial in which I sometimes mentally cast him, poured, stirred, asked, 'Milk? Sugar?' and proffered cup and saucer. It was because, I found myself thinking again, he had none of the outward attributes of power – height, sternness of feature or manner – and because, in some way, power really did not suit him at all, that his actual power so impressed – and maddened me.

'You look baffled, Prentis. As you say, it can be a torment not knowing things.'

I had confronted this formidable man who now was offering me coffee and Lincoln Creams. It did not seem such a daring act.

Quinn sipped his coffee. Through the glass panel I caught a brief glimpse of the office – Eric, Vic and O'Brien hunched at their desks like guinea-pigs in some controlled experiment.

The fly circled in towards the desk and settled on the plate of biscuits. We looked at it closely for some seconds and then, as if agreed on something, at each other.

'Tell me, Prentis – forgive me for not asking for so long – how is your father?'

24

I am amazed at the resignation, the composure of some of Dad's fellow inmates at the hospital. In my two years' visiting I have got to know several of them quite well. When I have sat out with Dad on the bench and walked back with him to the terrace and the wicker chairs, it is almost like returning to some haven of civilization after an interlude in the barren wilds. We sit, like old soldiers on a verandah, reflecting on lost glories. The ward windows catch the evening sun until it sinks behind the trees and the boundary wall. The shadows creep along the terrace. Inside, all the chores of the day have been done – meals served, drugs administered, bed linen changed, the ward floors swept and cleaned. The day staff wait to be relieved by the night staff, and Simpson, the ward orderly – who nods familiarly to me, as if I am just another member of the strange club for which he acts as steward – comes out to smoke away his last few minutes of duty. There is peace, order, stability – like nowhere else. And it seems to me that this is because here all the harm has been done; no one can be harmed any more.

They do not look like rebels, these figures in their

maroon dressing-gowns and faded bath-robes, like men who have trespassed beyond the bounds of sanity and been penned up for their pains. I have been thinking what would happen if some of those red-faced men with their cigars at the golf course (relaxed and at peace in a different way, and only members of another sort of club) were to be picked up by some giant hand and placed in one of these hospital wards. How they would scream and squeal and kick and be outraged. I would half like to be that giant hand. But these men, in their wicker chairs, they sit as if they are past argument, and even secretly thankful for something.

In the hospital everything goes in circles, or in irreversible regressions. Simpson, for example, used once to be a hospital inmate himself – not in Dad's hospital but another. When the time came for him to be discharged, he could find no other environment conducive to his peace of mind save that of a hospital and no other work save that of a hospital orderly. But the proximity of his job to his former condition naturally made it easy for him to slip back into it. So, for fifteen years, Simpson has been living in an ambiguous world in which he is sometimes patient, sometimes hospital employee, and even now, on occasion, instead of leaving the hospital at night for his bed-sit, he will nestle beneath the covers of one of the empty beds in the ward, and no one seems to mind. Simpson does not mind, himself. He is fifty-eight, wiry-haired, with leathery, unchanging features. He looks at you with a fixed, capable stare, like some servant of bygone days who would defend to the last his right to be no more than an underling.

Then there is Des. Des, who of all the occupants of Dad's ward I talk to most and who most takes the role of the one who 'keeps an eye' on Dad for me when I am not there. Des was once a Merchant Navy officer and entered the hospital nine years ago as a result of a head injury received in an accident at sea. On recovering, he applied to the relevant authorities for compensation and a disability pension. The authorities replied that the accident had been caused by Des's own negligence and he was therefore ineligible for compensation. Des denied his negligence and proposed to contest the matter. The response to this – even after Des's discharge from the hospital – was that the evidence of a man whose mental faculties were in question was inadmissible. For four years Des strove to have his claim upheld. The worry and exasperation involved induced recurrences of mental illness, thus strengthening the position of those judging his case. The constant questioning of his sanity in time dislodged it. He returned to the hospital for longer and longer periods, which eventually merged into a permanent residence in which his hope of receiving justice receded irrecoverably into the never-never. Now he sits on the terrace, like someone relieved at last of some burdensome misconception, and talks on these gentle summer evenings, without a trace of bitterness, of that other man, not himself at all, who by now has command of his own ship . . .

This gradual drifting back of discharged patients is a regular occurrence. Newly admitted patients are put into four wards which are for short stays only and from which, in theory, patients are sent out again into the world, wholly cured. In fact, a fair number of these released patients return, and this second visit is already a sign, not so much of incomplete cure, but that they have found the hospital atmosphere amenable and beguiling, they have formed a dependence. Other, longer visits follow the second one; with each, the probability of yet further visits becomes stronger; until they begin to live more out of than in the normal world, and, as with Des, permanent residence becomes inevitable. The hospital accepts this pattern. It is even embodied in its internal structure. For, apart from the two male and two female admission wards, there are, for each sex, five other wards which, broadly speaking, mark off the decline of any given patient. A patient who makes successive returns is gradually passed down the series of wards – first into those where residence can only winkingly be termed temporary; then into those where the prospect of never leaving the hospital is an unspoken certainty; then into those where the outside world ceases to exist, even as a concept. The passage through the wards, as through the mouth of a lobster-pot, is, almost without exception, one-way only. For some reason, the wards, which are normally referred to simply as A, B, C, D and so on, were once given by some euphemist the sweet-sounding names of flowers and trees ('Acacia', 'Anemone' etc). There is a joke in the hospital that the 'G' in the case of the last male and female wards ('Gladiolus' and 'Geranium') really stands for 'Gone Completely'.

Dad is in 'Eucalyptus'. It is more than halfway along the floral procession of wards (past the still hopeful and, in Dad's case, briefly visited 'Chrysanthemum' and 'Dahlia') and therefore past the point where rescue is likely. But they do not seem alarmed, these men in their dressing-gowns. They smoke, offer cigarettes and flick the ash off their knees like ordinary people. And, above all, they do not seem to beg release from the perpetual circles of their 'conditions'; they have ceased to try to escape. I have enjoyed these men's company – often silent or obscure, but pleasantly unpredictable and strangely free from every-day anxiety – as much as, if not more than anyone else's. More than Vic and Eric at the office, with their persistent chatter (which is only mine reciprocated) of cars and hire-purchase schemes and of (*they* should worry) getting nowhere at work.

Sometimes it strikes me that this agreeable impression is all a tremendous mistake. Sometimes I reflect that these men are ill; inside, they are in torment, they have terrible problems. I think of how little perhaps I know (though it has become familiar enough to me over the months) of the hospital; of what horrors there might be in 'Fuchsia' and 'Gladiolus' or even behind other, unmentioned and out-of-the-way doorways. And I think of the asylums of old in which the mad were locked away from view like concealed sins; of how these visitors, even now, who appear to flock in so readily on Sundays, perhaps fret and pull against the chain which ties them to the family monster and to an insidious nether-world of nightmares; of how the hospital staff, some of whom, it is true, are decidedly eccentric, manage to stop themselves, amidst all this derangement, from being infected by madness, of how they make the transition after work to the normal world of wives and children. All this gentle liberalism ('no doors are locked – patients are free to come and go'), all this atmosphere, on the terrace of 'Eucalyptus', of tranquillity and strange immunity, even the country-garden rose beds and lawns and rhododendron clumps, which now and then infuse you with a sense of inviolable idyll – all of it perhaps is a lie. But then, can the flowers and the trees lie?

Quite often I play chess with Des, on a fold-up wooden

table on the terrace. Whatever has happened to Des's mind, it is perfectly adept at chess, for he usually beats me. We sit on opposite sides of the table and Dad sits, looking blankly on, between us, as if we have given him the duty of umpire, and now and then we say, keeping up a pretence, 'Dad' (for Des uses that word too as if to show he and I have the same interests at heart) 'where shall I move? Which is the best move? The rook or the bishop?' And we imagine that when a move is successful it is Dad's advice that has brought it about. Sometimes I get so absorbed with the game – not just as a means of whiling away the visiting hours but with the game itself and being there on the terrace – that the official time for visitors to leave comes before I am aware of it, and Des has to preserve the position of the pieces for another day. When I show a reluctance to stop, and even to leave at all, Des, and Simpson too, occasionally wink at me, as much as to say, 'We understand.'

When I play chess with Des I think: a sane man, a man labelled insane cheerfully engrossed in the same activity when there should exist between us an uncrossable boundary line. Sanity? Insanity? Terrible problems? No, their problems are over. And when Des starts to ramble (for occasionally he starts to ramble, like a true hospital inmate), when he starts to speak of that other man, the master of the merchant vessel *Eucalyptus*, I think, no, it is not madness which is locked up and concealed like a crime, but something concealed behind madness. It was Des himself who, one day when Dad had been not long in his ward, came up to me and said, tapping his nose, 'You know the meaning of "Eucalyptus"? – "Well-hidden".'

But all these observations and reflections (you are

wrong if you think I am normally a thoughtful man – it is just something brought on by this urge to write things down) I do not make at all about Dad. I only make them about the hospital at large, as if about some abstract proposition. With Dad, despite the regularity of my visits and the continual silence in which we sit, there seems no time for thought or detachment. It is true, with every visit the more likely it becomes that nothing will change, that that silence will be never-ending. And yet each time I cannot help feeling, *this time* he will speak, and each time is special and urgent. Very often, when I come home afterwards, rather than that strange, lingering calm of the hospital, it is tension I feel; I tremble as if I have been involved in some immense struggle. For perhaps that is what they are, my meetings with Dad. His silence against my wish to hear him speak. We face each other like antagonists across a table (a different sort of chess, this), and one of us must crack first.

Do you recognize me? Answer me.

Is he doing it all to punish me?

I don't believe it can go on for ever. I don't believe they will send Dad on to 'Fuchsia' and then to 'Gladiolus'. If he endured the Château Martine (you were tortured, weren't you Dad? but you came through it) surely he will not yield to this. But only today I thought: perhaps it is by the self-same method he held out then as now: by keeping silent. And who can say that that is not the reason for Dad's present plight. Maybe what happened long ago at the Château Martine was so terrible as to have delayed effect thirty years later; and maybe while he sits on the wooden bench or on the wicker chair, amidst these innocent, therapeutic surroundings, he is really reliving endlessly – is it possible? – the torture of another time and place.

Sunday. The cedar tree. It was on my lips today to say, 'You knew X, didn't you? Who was he?' What stops me? Is it the fear of seeing Dad's face suddenly split with real pain? The fear of not being able to bear that?

The fountain was playing on the ornamental pond. We walked back to where the others sat like infinitely sagacious spectators on the terrace. All I said was: 'I shan't be here on Wednesday, Dad. I am going to see Mr Quinn.' (Now I know why I fixed on Wednesday. So Marian won't know. She'll believe I've gone to see Dad as usual. I'm not going to tell Marian I'm going to Quinn's.) 'He's invited me to his home.' As if Dad should answer, 'Ah yes, Mr Quinn, how kind of him.' 'He's going to tell me everything.' (Or rather, I didn't say that – only in my head. And nor did I say: 'Unless you tell me first.')

'So till next Sunday then.'

The bell was going for visitors to leave.

'Don't expect me on Wednesday.'

I left Dad on the terrace, with Des, Simpson and the others, and as I looked back, his still figure – that strong, intrepid, noble figure – seemed suddenly quite forlorn, as if I were leaving him for good.

25

And when I got home I took out Dad's book and dipped straight into it (those final chapters), with scarcely a word, not even an ill-tempered one, to Marian and the kids . . .

Marian is sulky and smouldering with silent resentment. Another Sunday has passed by – another beautiful sunny Sunday – and once again we haven't gone out, because I have taken the car and spent the afternoon with Dad. Yes, I know what she would say, if she had half the chance, about our 'wasted' Sundays. That I am the one who has this thing – or used to have – about going out into the open, about the countryside. I am the one who wants fresh air and hates skulking indoors. Yes, yes. As I turn the pages of Dad's book I have to brush aside a momentary vision of the weekends we used to have. Marian and I stripping hurriedly in the ferns. Wasps in the picnic basket.

Tonight we are unusually quiet and by ourselves. The kids are having a special treat tomorrow: they are going on a school outing to Chessington Zoo. They have to be away sharply, and this has given us the excuse for sending them early to bed. It's nearly ten now, and we ourselves could have an early night. But you know those Sunday evenings, when the weekend has been a failure and you're conscious that tomorrow is Monday, and you just try to mark time. The evenings are long and light; and there's just a hint of something magic in the sky which only now, when it's too late, do you notice, and which says: Fools! What do you want to go to sleep for, only to wake up for work? Marian has been pottering in the garden, and now she's going round with her plastic watering-can, watering her house-plants. I can hear her muttering to the peperomias and the sweetheart vine: 'Here you are then – I expect you're thirsty. There, that's better. We want to make you grow up big and strong, don't we?' I think she kisses them goodnight. It makes me jealous. I watch her through the open door of the living-room, bending over the rack of plants in the hall. She wears a pair of faded jeans and a thin, short-sleeved top that stops inches from her waist. I think: if she put down the watering-can and I put down my book we could lock up the house and go to bed and make love, hotly and deliberately, and lie awake for a while afterwards. Then everything would be clear and resolved between us. But we haven't made love of any sort for weeks. Instead, Marian makes love to the house-plants. '. . . we want to keep those nice green glossy leaves . . .' I watch her through the doorway. There is something less provocative than disturbing about that chink of bare flesh above her jeans.

. . . The Gestapo officers, despite their air of icy effi-
ciency, were all nervous. They knew they were conducting operations which at any moment might be cut short
by the arrival of the Americans or by the command to

withdraw. Every so often in these last few days, when the wind was right, we had heard the distant sound of shell-fire. This was a factor in my favour. But it worked both ways. The nervousness of the Germans might make them act with ruthless haste.

As we drove, we had to pass, some of the way, along the Belfort road where bedraggled sections of German divisions were already retreating. There was irony here (not greatly felt at the time): an army in retreat and one, self-important staff-car determinedly conveying a single prisoner. The driver sounded his horn to clear a way through the lines of battered trucks, field-kitchens, commandeered wagons and lumbering men. The two officers in the front seat visibly stiffened and, doubtless for my benefit, put on an air of not acknowledging what was happening. I sat between two guards. I had been handcuffed but my feet were free. At every halt, junction and slow section of road, I had wild thoughts of knocking one of the guards aside, crashing through the locked car door and running for it. But I knew that even if I got free of the car, in twenty yards I would have as many bullets in my back.

I did not need to be told we were heading for the Château Martine. I thought to myself: when we get within a certain distance they will blindfold me. But I already had a mental picture (how well it was to serve me later) of the roads and the lie of the land around the Château and Combe-les-Dames. I had got to know the area with Mathieu at the time when that ambitious plan had been formed, then shelved, to organize a mass-escape of the Château's prisoners. The Château Martine was where the SS now held 'priority' captives. Not ordinary Maquisards who had little to impart before being shot, but operators with special information and 'intelligence value'. A British agent was for them a real prize. Before me lay the fate that every agent knows may await him and which he tries to push to the back of his mind. Capture, interrogation . . . execution.

I had nothing to give away which, in German hands, could possibly alter the course of the war. But I knew enough about the overall pattern of resistance activities, about resistance cooperation with the Allies and even about the specific tactical objectives of the British and Americans to lend a possible sting to the German retreat and claim unnecessary extra lives. I also knew the whereabouts of four other British agents. I could not make mathematical calculations on the importance of my information. I was unlike the general in the field who consciously estimates and anticipates so much loss of life, so much damage to equipment for the sake of an overall victory, and therefore wittingly yields so much to his enemy. The spy's duty is to tell nothing, no matter how slight the strategic value of what he knows.

Sure enough, after we turned off the Belfort road, the blindfold came out. One of the officers said, in German and in English, 'Can you see?' And, to test the point, a pistol barrel struck me hard under the chin without warning.

I could tell we were climbing up into the hills, away from the river. The Château was only a matter of four kilometres away. It got cooler. I had dried out a good deal after my night in the water tank, but my clothes were still damp and I began to shiver. At the same time, with the blindfold on, the movement of the car round the hillside bends was making me nauseous. At length we took a turn and drove along a straight level stretch of road – the Château drive (between, as I remembered it, an avenue of chestnut trees). There was a crunching of gravel; the car wheeled and stopped. Barked orders and the noise of stamping boots. The officers in front and the guard on my left got out. Then the remaining guard, grasping me by my handcuffed arms and my collar, pulled me roughly through the right-hand door. I guessed we were in the courtyard of the Château.

There was a clipped '*Nehmen Sie ihn heraus!*' And I was dragged by the pair of guards across a few yards of gravel and through a door which I heard closed and locked behind us. Then to the left along a short, flagged passage, through another door, apparently manned by a guard with keys; along a corridor, wooden-floored and narrow (I felt myself squeezed between my two guards and heard their tunics brushing against the walls); sharply to the right (all these details I was making a conscious effort to remember), perhaps through a hundred and eighty degrees; through another door, heavy and narrow, and, again, unlocked, opened and relocked by a separate guard, and down a flight of stone steps. The steps took me completely by surprise. The two guards, who could no longer walk abreast of me, half let me tumble by my own weight and half dragged me, my legs tripping against the stone. All the time they had said nothing, except to the guard at the top of the steps, who merely replied, '*Drei – auf der linken Seite.*'

At the foot of the steps I heard the click of a switch and, even behind my blindfold, sensed an electric light come on. We moved on several yards down another flagged, musty-smelling passage. A third guard seemed to come from somewhere. Then a door was opened to my left – a door with a slow, ominous creak, like every true cell door – and I was thrust inside. I fell against a rough brick wall. My guards began to beat me up at once; not, it is true, a severe beating-up, but bad enough. Then my blindfold, which had already slipped, was pulled away. I had time to take in that I was in a windowless cellar with mould-covered walls, empty of furniture and with a heavy, metal-barred door, and that the only light came from the electric light in the corridor. Then the door was slammed in my face, a lock turned, bolts drawn. I heard the guards' boots down the corridor, watched the band of light under the door disappear. Then there was nothing – absolute darkness (I might as well have still been blindfolded), and a moist, permeating smell that was strangely familiar.

I thought to myself (it is strange how I scarcely felt the injuries of my beating-up – my one instinct was to think fast): they do not have much time themselves – they won't lose any with me. At any moment I will be hauled out for interrogation. But it was a long while before anything happened. I say 'a long while', but I had no real way of measuring time. My wrist-watch had been taken from me (not that I would have been able to see it) along with everything else save my clothes. Someone should make a study one day of the effects of a completely darkened room on one's ability to estimate and make judgements. I sat with my bruises. There were no sounds. The walls of an old French Château must be very thick. Sometimes I seemed to hear muffled voices and shouts and the sound of car motors from the direction I supposed the courtyard to be. I tapped the walls. No answering tap. They were indeed thick; or I had no neighbours. There was only one other way of putting this to the test. I groped till I felt the door, stood up and shouted at the top of my voice (stupidly, as I afterwards realized), '*Il n'y a personne?*' No reply; but almost immediately, to my surprise, light appeared beneath the door and someone came along the corridor from the left. My door was opened. A round-faced, small-eyed German like an outsize schoolboy stood in front of me. He held a long stick. '*Qu'est-ce que vous voulez?*' he said in an atrocious accent and, before I could answer, struck me hard across the chest with the stick (it was actually a polished truncheon, made for the purpose). I crumpled against the wall. '*Vous avez faim?*' he added (words which I did not understand till later), then locked the door on me. The electric light went out. I did not attempt to utter another sound after this.

It had been perhaps four in the afternoon when I was deposited in my cell. After what seemed at least three hours, I heard the noise of opening doors and then of footsteps descending the steps down which I had been previously dragged. The light was switched on and showed through the crack under my door. I was already learning to make use of that thin, fleeting beam as a means, however feeble, of discerning something of my cell. The footsteps stopped; a door some ten yards away on the other side of the corridor was unlocked and opened, and, to judge by the sounds, someone dragged out. There was much 'rausing' and 'schnelling', then footsteps and scuffling going away; the outer door being shut and locked; then silence again.

This silence seemed more set to last than the first. I guessed it was now night. I sat propped against one of the walls. The sheer pressure on the nerves of waiting for something to happen was beginning to tell. I was cold and nearly every bone in my body seemed to have taken a sharp knock. I took consolation by reminding myself that I had spent the previous night in a water tank. I reflected that they were deliberately letting me stew before they questioned me, and therefore I should stop myself from stewing. I began to combat negative thoughts by methodically exploring my cell with my handcuffed hands. I started at a corner near the door and worked round in a clockwise direction, beginning at floor level, working up as far as my hands would reach, then down again, and so on. Then I began on the floor, working from the wall furthest from the door.

My hands confirmed what my eyes had briefly seen when the blindfold had been removed: a brick room about eight feet square, containing nothing and with no outlet save the door. The floor was strewn with a thick mixture of what I took to be dust, grit and sawdust. The smell of the sawdust, and of damp wood generally, was what pervaded the room, but why this smell was so peculiarly familiar I could not tell. The brickwork of the walls was rough and coated with dust and cobwebs. Here and there, there were sections where the mortar had crumbled between the courses. My fingers groped, in vain, in the gaps. But they found something that, in due course, was to prove invaluable. Sticking into one of the walls, high up, was a single, long, straight-sided, rust-covered nail. I made a note of the position of this nail. By persistent efforts, I managed to pull it free, and placed it, lengthwise, in one of the mortarless gaps in the brick courses, for safe keeping.

I must have fallen into a deep sleep. I was woken by my door being unbolted, by shouts and the entry of two guards (not those of the day before) into my cell. I suffered the exquisite pain of believing for a moment I was not where in fact I was. The guards pulled me on to my feet and I was shoved along the corridor. I thought to myself: the moment has come. But I also considered: better for it to happen like this, suddenly and even after having slept than to sit and wait for it. My body was stiff and ached cruelly. We took the same route, in reverse, as the day before: along the corridor, where now, with my eyes uncovered, I noticed, on either side, other doors, doubtless to cells like my own; up the stone steps, and through the outer door, on the other side of which a guard was posted. Here, for the first time, daylight, subdued and indirect though it was, stabbed my eyes. I was marched round a corner to the left and then, not left again, which would have accorded with my route of entry the day before, but right – and face to face, all at once, with a magical vision. We were in a narrow hallway, painted in delicate duck-egg blue, with gilt cornices and hung with two or three gilt-framed pictures. At the end of this hallway – about eight yards ahead – was a tall, stately, deep-casemented window opening on to a view of a classical French garden bathed in the light of a September dawn: terraces, urns, statuary, long ornamental ponds between lawns silvered with dew; a low sun looming over misty trees. As unreal as some painting by Watteau or Claude.

We walked towards this mirage, the sun streaming through the glass on to our faces, and I had a brief, preposterous notion that I was going to be flung into it. But I was jerked abruptly to the right, round a corner. During the second or two in which we passed the window I had time to notice that the ground sloped away quite steeply from the back of the Château, that the window was several feet above ground level and that below it was a long, balustraded terrace which at least one sentry was patrolling.

We climbed up two flights of grand, carved stairs and emerged on to a landing in front of an ornate double door behind which, I instinctively knew, were my interrogators. An officer, whom I recognized as the dark-haired, fat-cheeked officer present at my capture, was lounging on the landing, his black tunic unbuttoned, a coffee cup in his hand. He looked at me with distaste and motioned to one of the guards. I was taken along a side corridor and ushered, almost considerately, into a cubicle containing a large marble wash basin, a mirror and a lavatory. In the mirror I became aware of the filth – dust and dried blood – that had collected on my face. The sentry removed my handcuffs. '*Waschen Sie sich.*'

Marian is finishing watering her plants. She straightens up and rubs a palm on her hip. She does not know I am looking at her. She is a creature undergoing scientific scrutiny: her sandy hair, slightly hunched shoulders, her slim, almost too slim body, her exposed midriff. She turns and catches my clinical stare. A bewildered look crosses her face. I return my eyes to the book and do not look up again until she speaks. 'I'm going to have a bath,' she says, as if I've implied she's unclean.

After I had washed (it seemed my handcuffs were not going to be replaced), the guard jostled me back towards the double doors, which had been partly opened. The second guard was standing on the landing. He jerked his head as a sign to his companion, who shoved me through the doors and pulled them shut behind me.

Here description must be blurred. Not through any weakness of recollection, but because events themselves at the time were blurred. The first step towards breaking the resistance of a spy is to confuse and disorientate him, and deprivation, isolation, hunger, sleeplessness, as well as the spy's own ignorance of the next move of his captors, normally achieve this – even before other methods are employed. The room into which I was pushed was large, thick-carpeted, with a marble fire-place set in one wall, and the wooden scrollwork and gilt which characterized the corridors and staircase. Another door, in one corner, led off it. Blinds were drawn over the windows and although light filtered in, electric lights, set in chandeliers, were switched on. Before me was a large, leather-topped desk, strewn with papers, and behind it, sitting in heavily upholstered chairs, were the fat-cheeked officer and a second officer, in the uniform of an SS colonel, with neat grey hair and a long, delicate, almost scholarly face, like that of some amiable civil servant. Up to now my journey up from the cell had had a strangely reassuring quality, as if nothing worse were going to happen to me than happens to some refractory schoolboy. But I noticed that on the small wooden chair in which, if I was lucky, I would be told to sit, there were dark stains of blood, and the chair itself was placed on a large piece of canvas material, over the carpet, on which there were more obvious stains of blood, and, if my nostrils did not deceive me, urine . . .

'Do you want one?'
'What?'

'A bath.'

'Why?'

'I mean, do you mind if I take all the hot water?'

'No, no . . .'

She stands in the doorway, like some subordinate, waiting to be told she is dismissed.

. . . I was to sit in that chair, on that piece of filthy canvas, many times in the ensuing few days. How many times exactly, I could not say, nor for what duration, nor with what intervals in between; nor, were it not for certain regular daily procedures, could I have said at the time that what was involved was merely a matter of days, not weeks, months – an epoch. My recollection compresses into a series of dream-like, constantly recurring impressions: the darkness and silence of the cell punctuated (as you sank into exhaustion) by the tramping of boots, lights, shouts, the rasping of locks and bolts and the slam of doors; the journey, on which your own legs could scarcely convey you, along the passage-way, up the steps, along the upper corridor, past that incredible window, which every time became more and more like an illusion; the staircase, the double doors, the guard shoving you into the cubicle, and that persistent command: *'Waschen Sie sich'*. Perhaps there is much about my days at the Château which I simply do not remember. They say that you only recall what is pleasant. Or perhaps the truth is that certain things defy retelling.

When grey-hair and fat-cheeks had finished with me that first time, I was taken back down not, at first, to my cell, but to the room at the end of the cell corridor where the podgy German with the truncheon officiated. I was detained here for perhaps an hour.

What was it like, Dad? What was it really like?

Dumped back in my cell, I was roused again, almost immediately, this time by a general activity in the corridor. What was about to take place was a regular event which occurred every morning; for the first time I was to see some of my fellow captives. In the corridor the cell doors were being opened and the prisoners were automatically forming a single file. I counted seven, excluding myself. Some of them were hardly able to stand. The doors to the cells either side of my own were unopened. I assumed from this and my previous unanswered tapping that they were unoccupied. Each of the prisoners in the corridor held a battered metal can – obviously provided for his needs of nature. I had none myself, but one was to be 'issued' to me during the proceedings that followed.

When all the prisoners were lined in the corridor a command was given by one of the guards and we shambled forwards towards the exit steps. I was last in the line and was denied, for the moment, the opportunity to look for faces I might know. We passed through the door at the top of the steps and then turned left, along the passage-way through which I had been bundled, blindfolded, on my arrival. I made a mental note of everything. From the outset, and as the only conceivable positive course in the circumstances, I had resolved on escape.

We filed through another doorway, at which guards were posted, turned right, and suddenly emerged into the fresh, blinding air of the Château courtyard. A staff-car, two motorcycles with side-cars and a light truck were parked on the gravel. Sentries were posted at the gateway into the courtyard, and, dotted around the courtyard itself, standing casually but with rifles at the ready, were soldiers of the SS – I counted over a dozen – looking at us with an air of somewhat listless mockery. Doubtless, this was their morning's entertainment.

I copied the actions of the prisoners in front of me. The line moved along to the left, flanked now by several guards with pointed rifles. We passed in front of a pump, below which was a large, metal-grilled drain. As each prisoner reached the pump he emptied the contents of his can down the drain with the aid of a sluicing from the pump. My lack of a can caused ribald laughter amongst our onlookers. The line then moved on towards a long, low trough, filled with water and fed by another pump. The file broke up and we took up places on either side. The trough itself was not clean, but every man, before washing (that was clearly the purpose of the trough), dipped his face in the water and drank deeply. I did so, without hesitation, myself. I could not help reflecting on the apparent obsession of our captors with a token cleanliness. We were given a full five minutes to scrub and rinse ourselves, and the touch of the water, though it stung and stabbed at bruises and scars, gave a sort of bitter pleasure.

I had an opportunity now to study my comrades. They were a pitiful sight. Dressed in ragged clothes, hollow-eyed, unshaven, and bearing, without exception, the marks of heavy beatings – if not of more precise and calculated injuries. Some seemed so feeble it was a wonder they had made it to the courtyard. One, in particular, was unable to wash himself and had to be helped by his neighbours. His nose had been sliced and all the fingers on his right hand systematically crushed.

As we bent over the washing trough the guards encircled us and it was obvious that talking was forbidden. But while stooping low, and with the noise of slopping water and the pump, it was possible to exchange a few words that went unnoticed. French was the only language I heard amongst the prisoners; as far as I knew, I was the only Britisher at the Château. I found myself opposite a stocky figure with a ragged beard whom I vaguely recognized as one of the group from Dôle. Without any preliminary introductions, he whispered through the cupped hands with which he washed his face:

'You shouted last night.'

'Shouted?'

'When they brought you in – "*Il n'y a personne?*" If we make a noise in the cells we get no food. That is the rule. We will not eat now till tomorrow.'

He spoke without the slightest trace of friendship. I was beginning to realize that in prisons there is as much suspicion and enmity between the prisoners as between captives and captors. But I understood at last the odd question of the truncheon-wielder.

'You are in one of the back cells – in the dark?'

'Yes.'

'You're lucky.'

It was not clear to me why being confined in the dark was lucky. But with the slightest movement of his head my neighbour indicated the base of the Château wall on the side of the courtyard where we had emerged. There were tiny, semicircular, barred openings at and (because of a sort of gutter which ran round the perimeter of the courtyard) just below ground level. I realized that these must mark the row of cells on the opposite side of the corridor to my own. While my own cell, perhaps, adjoined the outer wall of the Château, these adjoined the courtyard and were equipped with these small apertures which allowed light to enter.

'They look in on us like animals in cages. They watch us all the time.'

A guard drew close; we had to cease whispering for a moment.

'You have visited *"le goret"*?'

Again, I followed a slight movement of my companion's head. Our chubby acquaintance from the room at the end of the cell corridor had emerged into the courtyard and was sauntering up and down. *'Goret'* is French for 'piglet'. An apt word.

'Yes.'

'Too bad,' he said, without feeling. He was evidently trying to gauge my qualities as a prisoner. I vaguely knew who he was, and he, most likely, had a clearer idea who I was. Many Frenchmen I had met had an ingrained distrust of captured Englishmen. They believed that the Gestapo treated them more leniently.

We spoke no more. My companion's last remark had been detected. He was seized by the shoulder, knocked with a rifle butt, and when he fell, kicked several times in the ribs. It could just as easily have been me.

After washing, we were made to form into a line again. By this time another ten or so prisoners, with their cans, had been led out from another wing of the Château towards the first pump. So we were not the only ones.

It was clear we were not to be returned to our cells directly. At a command our party was made to parade in single file, several times, round the perimeter of the courtyard. This, perhaps, had the spurious purpose of 'exercise', but was really only a sadistic diversion. We were forced to march in mock drill fashion, arms swinging high, at a pace neither too slow nor too fast. One of the guards even stood calling out the time: '*Links! . . . Links!*' Any failure to keep in step, to maintain the pace or to hold the head up was immediately dealt with by blows and kicks. For some of our number, who were tottering even as they stood by the washing trough, this 'exercise' was torture. I wondered how long it would be before I was like them. In such a condition you would not be able to escape.

But, as yet relatively fresh, I was able to take in, during this bizarre ritual, the scene around me. There was something cruelly incongruous about the Château itself – its solid, cream-stuccoed walls, its tall windows capped with rococo scrollwork, its little French corner turrets, its air of tranquillity and gracious, harmonious living. Up above, on the weathered tiles of the roof, which was bathed in sunlight, there were even doves preening and cooing. And, all around, I could sniff (as though I hadn't been living amidst it for the last four weeks) the tangy, woody, late-summer air of Eastern France. These things seemed impossible. It was the same inside: the carved woodwork, the gilt, the elegant stairways – and, below, the dungeons. As we paraded round, I noticed that four or five officers, one of whom was 'grey-hair', had emerged from the portion of the Château which lay opposite the arched gateway. Here there were large glass doors and a series of shallow, wide steps. They stood at the top of the steps or just inside the glass doors, smoking cigarettes and coughing behind raised hand. They looked at the proceedings in the courtyard like inspectors approving some project in hand.

'*Schauen Sie geradeaus!*' I was struck sharply on the side of the face.

One section of the courtyard wall, to the right of the gateway, I could not fail to notice. On it there were smears of dried blood, and on the ground beneath, darker, denser blood-stains. The wall itself was pitted with bullet marks.

We were now halted and made ready for being led back to the cells. First, each man had to collect his can from beside the first pump. I acquired one of my own in the following way. Since I was the last in the line and had brought no can with me up to the courtyard, I was empty-handed. One of the guards, however, snatched away the can belonging to the prisoner with the crushed hand and presented it, almost with courtesy, to me. '*Prenez!*' he said. Then added, in German: '*Er hat die letzte Scheisse gehabt.*' Guffaws arose from the other guards. Later that day (if day it still was), shots were heard – the first of several fusillades I was to hear from my cell – and at the next morning's 'muster' the prisoner with the crushed hand was missing.

(I remembered a story Mathieu had once told me about another Gestapo establishment in Dijon, which I had thought was a joke: 'They only have so many cans. So when there are not enough to go round they shoot one of the prisoners.')

We were now marched back to the cells. I was anxious to know if they would return us to the same cells from which we came. They did – now and on subsequent occasions. They made a mistake here.

After only a brief respite in my cell, I was dragged up again by the guards to grey-hair and fat-cheeks; then to '*le goret*'s' room; then back to my cell for another brief period; then to grey-hair and fat-cheeks again. And so on.

At some time later – how long I could not say – I found myself mercifully left to languish. It was then that I heard the shots from the courtyard. I was so numb and fatigued that I heard them almost with indifference. I slept – not the deep, oblivious sleep of exhaustion, but a fitful sleep, broken by the noise of scuffling in the corridor and screams from '*le goret*'s' room. Then – at dawn again, as it turned out: grey-hair and fat-cheeks.

During those twenty-four hours, as my neighbour at the water-trough had predicted, we received no food – at least, I received none. On the second day a bowl of something was shoved into my cell. An unspeakable swill. We were given no drinking-water save what we gulped at the trough.

At the next muster in the courtyard my companion murmured under his breath: 'They shot Fernand' (the name, I gathered, of the prisoner with the broken fingers). 'Now he is out of his misery. Sometimes they shoot you in the courtyard; sometimes they say, "Please, take a walk in the garden." Among the roses, a machine-gun . . .'

I could not help forming a dislike for this friend of mine and his grim brand of phlegm. His remarks did nothing to help morale, and I even suspected him of having some sort of double role. But then I realized that his way of seizing on me like a new boy and attempting to scare me was his means of gaining a little power and authority, and this in turn gave him the will to survive. A brief lesson in prison psychology.

Sometimes during these morning musters we would hear, on the air, the distant sound of shell-fire. Our captors put on unperturbed looks and so betrayed inward unease. The sound gave us all a flutter of hope, but, at the same time, if anything, it loaded the balance of fate against us. The chances of our captors abandoning the Château without first herding us all together and executing us were a thousand to one.

On the fourth morning (I believe it was the fourth morning) the Germans adopted a new ruse. In the courtyard, by the washing trough, we were told to strip. Our clothes were put in a heap. We were made to parade in the usual way, unclad, and were led back to our cells naked. From then on, at all times and in all circumstances, we were without clothes. A small matter, on top of so much; but of all the humiliations and cruelties – more intricate, more painful – we had to endure, none, I think, was more demoralizing, more appalling than this nakedness.

This was the pattern – but pattern is hardly the word – of our life at the Château. What remains? What more can be added? Memory provides its own, thankful censorship. If one dominant impression stays with me, it is that – the everyday man in everyday circumstances does not know what it means – of being absolutely in the power of another. This ought to be a condition of the utmost seriousness. But it is not. You feel yourself to be the mere pawn, the mere dehumanized toy that you are. Many times as I huddled naked in the dark in my cell, when even the redeeming will to escape had deserted me, I thought, nothing matters, I am in their hands: all this is a game . . .

I look up from the book. Outside, the long June evening has grown dim and I realize that for some time, in my absorption, I have been straining to read without a light. But it is as though I have been straining not so much against the dark but to discern some hidden things behind the words. I switch on the light. From upstairs I can hear the sounds of Marian's bath running and the noise of the water in the pipes. What happened in '*le goret*'s' room, and in those interrogation sessions with fat-cheeks and grey-hair? Why do I need to know these things – to eavesdrop on my Dad's suffering? So as to become like one of his tormentors? To become like Dad? With so much of Dad's book I have to struggle to make it real, to wrest it out of the story-book realm into the realm of fact. Because I know I could not have done half those things Dad did in France, and so for me it has always seemed not wholly real. And yet in these last chapters there is more of the flavour of reality, because there is also more mystery – and more misery. Why should that be? I can believe in these scenes of cruelty and deprivation. I can believe that they happened. Is that shocking? Sometimes they can actually seem one, that silent dummy in the hospital ward and that figure in his pitch-dark cell. And not only this, but because I believe in these passages, I can put myself into them, I can imagine myself in that dark cell, in those passage-ways, that courtyard. Why does it seem that I *know* that Château? So that sometimes in my mind – it is like this tonight – it almost seems that Dad and I are one too. But I must know everything. I must know every detail. So whatever Dad endured, I will know if I could endure it too; what is expected of me too.

But that is not the only mystery. There is the mystery of X. This only makes things more tangled and obscure. Dad doesn't mention him. He even says explicitly at one point: 'French was the only language I heard amongst the prisoners . . . the only Britisher at the Château.' Perhaps X was not there, or there but at a different time – or in some part of the Château where Dad would not have seen him. Perhaps it is all the work of my over-ripe imagination: X, 'Arthur', the golf course . . .

But I have been making notes while I have been reading – just as I would when going through one of Quinn's files at the office. I have been jotting down those words, those little additional comments, those inconsistencies, which most seem to draw me into the mystery – and closer to Dad:

I made a mental note of everything.
I only recall . . . there is much I simply do not remember.
Memory provides its own censorship.

From the outset I had resolved on escape . . .
. . . the redeeming will to escape . . .
. . . in such a condition you would not be able to escape.

The spy's duty is to tell nothing.
All this is a game.

. . . lawns silvered with dew . . . doves preening . . . tangy, woody, late-summer air . . .
. . . impossible . . . mirage . . . illusion . . .

. . . a way of gaining a little power and authority, and . . . in turn . . . the will to survive . . .
. . . absolutely in the power of another . . . in their hands
. . . mere pawn . . . mere dehumanized toy . . .

. . . of all the humiliations . . .

And now, suddenly, I think I am there –

. . . of all the humiliations and cruelties . . . none . . . was
more demoralizing, more appalling than this nakedness.

26

I close the book and return it to the shelf. I fold up the piece of paper on which I have been writing these notes and slip it into my pocket. I don't want Marian or the kids to discover it. I go up to the bathroom to get ready for bed.

Marian is lying in a foot or so of soapy water. Her skin is pink with the heat, and globules of sweat cover her face. She says 'Hello' uneasily and coyly. This is not because she reacts with modesty at being seen in the bath, but because when she is in the bath she is vaguely conscious of appearing ridiculous. She wears a plastic shower cap with a frill and likes to surround herself with all sorts of oils and lotions. 'Hello,' I return, and stand, looking down at her, by the edge of the bath. She peers up at me with the frozen look of someone anticipating some attack and scared to provoke that attack by making a move of defence. She lowers her chin and seems to be trying to draw her whole body beneath the water. In other circumstances and around the house generally she can act with indifference or resentment, but here she is cornered and has no choice but to plead innocence. Her breasts bob and glisten; just beneath the surface is the dark triangle between her legs. But my thoughts are neither aggressive nor lustful. I am thinking of Martin and Peter when they were very young. How I used to bathe them in a plastic baby-bath; how when I sat them in the water I used to think how tender, how pitiful their pink flesh was – even hot water would make them scream; how they used to look up with the same look as Marian now – uncertain, defenceless, compelled to trust – and how I used to think: 'Now they are at my mercy.'

'What are you looking at?' she says ineptly.

'You're all pink,' I say, equally ineptly.

And I have this sudden urge to wash my wife. To kneel down at the edge of the bath and – with the utmost tenderness – to run the soap and the bath-sponge over her body.

When I first knew Marian I used to meet her sometimes, at the end of the day, at the clinic where she worked as a physiotherapist. There were all these people, recovering from broken bones, with muscle defects and spinal problems, and there was this lovely, healthy girl instructing them. I used to watch them, doing exercises, through the glass doors. Most of the patients were elderly or middle-aged men, some of them solid, self-important types made to look foolish through sudden incapacity. I used to think: now they are having to learn to walk again and use their arms, like children. They used to worry about all sorts of things like bank overdrafts and making sure of their pensions; now they are all occupied with something as simple as getting their bodies to work. I could see their pent-up annoyance and frustration. But they obeyed Marian's instructions meekly and implicitly and looked at her as if they depended on her completely. I used to be amazed and jealous at Marian's power over her patients; even a little bit afraid of her because I thought that the power she exercised over them she would also wield over me. But when the time came it was quite different. I was surprised by her passivity and by the way her body became something offered up completely to me. I suppose that is what happens in love: you bare your breast and say, I am in your hands. And the first time we went to bed together I couldn't help thinking of those men, behind the glass doors, with their braces and crutches and sticks.

'It's hot in here,' I say, wiping my brow. Another stupid and pointless remark. Marian must see that I'm as bewildered as her. The room is full of vapour. Condensation streams off the bathroom tiles. We look at each other through a mist.

And later, in the bedroom, when I'm already in bed, with Dad's book propped before me, Marian comes in and there is a moment when once again she must be, fleetingly, naked. She has a bath-towel wrapped round her, tucked under her arms and coming down just over her hips. She bends down to dump some clothes on a chair and her bottom shows. I look, but it's not desire I feel. We haven't made love for weeks but it's not desire I feel, even though I felt it only an hour ago when she stood in the hall. She unwraps the towel. She doesn't wear a night-dress. It's hot. Outside, it's the sort of velvet mid-summer night in which no creature sleeps. She slips into her side of the bed. How tender, how pitiful. We used to get up to all those erotic games, now we are like a shy couple, starting over again. She is dusted with talc. Her skin smells like a baby. She says, 'When are you going to stop reading that book?' And I say, 'Soon. Quite soon.'

27

Before I went to sleep I thought: I was born in August 1945. I must have been conceived when Dad came home, after his escape, from France. Mum and Dad together in the autumn of '44. A honeymoon hotel amidst tangy, woody air. I am a product of those times and of all that happened in the Château Martine.

28

This Monday I didn't see Quinn at all at the office. He didn't even appear at his glass panel. Perhaps this was appropriate. Why should we make a point of bumping into each other when in a couple of days' time we are going to meet, so to speak, more strictly face to face? Or perhaps Quinn is unwilling to see me because he knows that very soon he has some confession to make. At any rate, Monday was a better day than usual. I didn't have to work late and I didn't come home with my customary headache and bad temper. The kids had been out all day on their school trip and were tired and amenable and because they had not come home at their normal time I did not have to suffer Martin's surveillance on my walk from the Tube.

Chessington Zoo, if you do not know it, is a sort of zoo with a funfair thrown in. There are whirligigs and a ghost-train. It makes no bones about what is implicit in most zoos – that they are places of entertainment rather than science, and that the dividing line between zoos and circuses is usually a thin one. Personally, I don't care much for this circus element, but I am very fond of zoos as such.

You can learn a lot from animals. About people, I mean, not just about animals. You can sometimes learn more about people from looking at animals than you can from looking at people. Take my advice: spend a few hours attentively in a zoo, then go and sit in a crowded pub. Or take a ride on the Tube. And there is something gratifying – something calming and reassuring, I can't explain it – simply about being amongst animals. One of my favourite places – let me recommend it – is the Small Mammal House at Regent's Park.

Yes, I know there is a falseness, a contradiction about the very concept of these animal playgrounds. Like golf courses and public commons: natural and artificial at the same time, wild-but-tame. But perhaps this is the way things must be now.

We were having a discussion along these lines at breakfast before the kids left. Or, rather, I was delivering a lecture to Martin and Peter. Parents had been asked by the teachers to provide their children not only with a packed lunch but with 'a little pocket-money' for the day. I doled them out a generous two pounds each. It was a way of securing their compliance. I could see all this money being spent on candy-floss and rides on dodgem-cars, and so I said: 'You won't forget to look at some animals too.' They looked puzzled – weren't they going to a zoo? But I could imagine them looking for a while at the leopards and antelopes, getting bored and then heading for the ghost-train. They wouldn't linger, contemplate the warm fur, think of the rustle in the undergrowth . . . And then I launched into this monologue about the function of zoos. 'You know, zoos aren't just places to go and have fun,' I began, 'they have a serious purpose too.' Phrases like 'serious purpose' were all right for Martin, but they go straight over Peter's head. I forgot about eating my breakfast. 'Zoos were originally set up, you see, as places to *study* animals . . .' And then I explained how in the nineteenth century when people started to live in big cities they also started to get interested in nature, as if it were something foreign, and zoos were an expression of this. This may all have been sheer bunk. I know nothing about the history of zoos or when the first zoos were founded. But I elaborated the point at length. I thought: how strangely you spend your time. Last night I was reading about my Dad's experiences at the hands of the Gestapo and sniffing Marian's talcumed body. Now I am propounding for my sons the growth of zoology in the nineteenth century. Half way through, I remembered that they no longer teach Nature Study as a subject in schools. 'So you see,' I concluded, 'animals are really kept in zoos so we can understand them scientifically.'

Peter looked lost. Martin frowned and introduced into his expression a sardonic cast which he has been cultivating ever since his coup with Dad's book. I could see that he thought what I was saying was so much grown-up claptrap. Worse – that he was actually going to take issue with me.

'But how can you,' he demanded, ' – when they're not the real thing?' And then he said something pithy and aphoristic which made me inwardly panic at the speed of his mental development and, more than this (there was a sharp gleam in his eye), at his psychological penetration.

'A lion in a cage isn't a real lion.'

'But it's not *practical*,' I blustered, 'to study – er – monkeys, when they're leaping about in the jungle.'

'So why not leave them alone?'

Do other fathers have this terror over the breakfast table, when they realize their sons are growing up to be smarter than them?

'But then you wouldn't be able to go out for days at the zoo, would you?' A weak argument. 'And you'd never know about lots of interesting animals.'

'Why should we have to know about them?'

All this was too clever by half. I thought, he will be saying next that keeping lions and monkeys in cages is cruel.

'Keeping animals in cages is cruel, Dad.'

I looked at him. So, it's cruel, eh? But I'd bet he'd still like a pet of his own.

'But if you didn't put them in cages you'd never get to see them.'

(For what else can you do these days, if you want to be close to nature, but put it in a cage?)

He paused for a moment.

'Yes you would. There are plenty of good programmes about animals – on *television*.'

I was outwitted, nonplussed. I looked helplessly round the room for inspiration. Marian had left the table and was in the kitchen. She was preparing packs of sandwiches, slices of swiss roll and chocolate biscuits for the boys to take with them. Martin's eyes were pinned on me. Peter was sitting, blinking and frowning, glancing now at me, now at his brother, daunted, once again, by Martin's audacity, and by this clash of words which he did not really understand. He looked, himself, like a little caged animal. Might he be on my side? And then, in desperation, an answer came – an answer which in fact I thought rather a neat one and too subtle for Martin, so I delivered it in a loud voice, for Marian to hear:

'But don't you think television is just another sort of cage?'

Martin stared at me blankly for a while. I thought: now I have silenced him. And then he said, as if this conversation about zoos were merely by the by: 'Dad – why do you walk in that funny way on your way home from the station?'

But in spite of this ignominious start Monday wasn't such a bad day. I had woken up with the thought: On Wednesday I will see Quinn; on Wednesday I will know; I can be patient till then. And it was this thought that restrained me, just as I was about to let fly at Martin. And then something Marian said to me as we saw the boys off on their trip jolted me out of my sulks and made me forget almost completely this breakfast episode. The boys had to be early at school, where a coach was coming for the zoo party, and since this coincided with the time of my departure for work we all got into the car and Marian drove us first to the school, then took me on to the station. At the school two coaches were parked already outside the gates. There were all these gabbling children with picnic bags and satchels and plastic water-bottles on straps slung over their shoulders. Teachers trying to make counts; mothers fussing and petting. I thought of evacuees in war-time. I thought of the anguish of parents frightened of bombs. Coach-crashes. Marian got out of the car with the boys and kissed them both on the top of the head. She gave Peter an extra kiss and a little pat on the bottom for good measure. She didn't walk across to the coach with them or wait to see them off. They had already spotted their friends and didn't want us around. She's a shrewd mother. I waved dutifully to one of the teachers, Mrs Thurleigh, who is always saying, as if it's her phrase for all occasions, that we have 'two bright boys'. (I never have the nerve to say to her, 'But there's something unnatural about them, isn't there?') Marian got back into the car and we waved through the window. And then, as we drove to the station, she said: 'Did you know you yelled out in your sleep last night? You said: "Is there anyone there?"'

29

. . . At night (but by 'night' I mean any period when I was shut up in the dark) I tried to identify the smell that pervaded my cell. It is strange how imprisonment affects the memory: the mind is confined as much as the body. I knew *what* the smell was: it was the smell of damp, partly rotten wood. But I did not know what kind of wood or where it was that I had smelt it, so distinctly, before. Another thing puzzled me. The air in my cell, though odorous and fully enclosed, was never fetid.

Then I made an important discovery.

In those snatches of exhausted sleep I would lie huddled at the foot of one of the walls. Once, lying against the wall opposite the door, I felt about my face a tiny but distinct trickle of air. Not only this, but borne on this faint draught was another, incredible but unmistakable smell: the smell of lavender.

I put my hand to the brickwork and began exploring the mortar joints. It was then that the identity of the first smell – the wood smell – came to me – and along with it a series of inferences which made my imagination and my heart race.

My grandfather on my mother's side had lived in a handsome eighteenth-century house not far from Winchester. It was equipped with cellars, accessible from within the house but with openings, covered with heavy cast-iron plates, at the foot of the outer walls, through which materials for storing could be passed. My grandfather still used one of the cellars for what was perhaps its original purpose – the storing of fire-wood. Nearby, there were extensive fruit orchards and my grandfather had a standing arrangement for supplies of logs. It was the smell of apple logs in my grandfather's cellar in Hampshire that I was smelling again in the Château Martine. As a child, staying with my grandparents during the summer, the cellars had always intrigued me. I liked to explore them and I regarded them as places of refuge whenever I had incurred adult displeasure. I was never frightened of them. Perhaps, in a remote way, I owe my ability to endure the Château to my boyhood experience. To have existed in those cells and to have suffered at the same time from claustrophobic fear of the dark would have been too much to bear. To me, the smell of apple wood in the dark (and this perhaps was why I could not place it, in such hostile surroundings) was the smell of sanctuary.

But this was not the time for nostalgia. My returning memory had highly practical implications. If my grandfather's Hampshire home had had openings in the exterior wall which connected to the cellars by a brick chute through which logs could be tipped, was it not possible that the same system applied in a Château in eastern France? Was it not possible that at some time the purpose of the cellar had been changed – or the cellar had become disused – and that the opening to the chute had been sealed up, inexpertly – by a wall of only single bricks perhaps? – from the inside? And the Germans, in converting it again to to a cell, had overlooked this? One begins to believe in strange, benevolent miracles of fate.

I set to work with the rusty nail I had extracted from the wall. It is perfectly true, not a mere adage, that hope gives you strength. By testing with the nail I ascertained that there was indeed an irregular section of brickwork, perhaps two feet across, slightly different in texture from the rest of the wall, and for which a different, weaker mortar had been used. Tapped with a knuckle, this section gave a more resonant sound.

I began immediately to scratch away at the mortar with the nail, close to where the air, through some unseen crack, was periodically infiltrating. Even as I did so I was hastily working out possibilities and precautions. When next my cell door was opened I must look quickly at this part of the wall to make a visual note of what I could only, so far, feebly gauge by touch. But if I did this I would draw the attention of the guards. I must therefore hide my work. But how? The latrine-can. This was about eighteen inches tall. Placed against the wall, it would hide some of the patch in question; as for the rest, I must make do. To conceal my chipping and scraping I must rub and scuff the area worked on with dirt from the cell floor. This would still show, but I could only hope the guards would not notice. To darken the mortar-dust made by my chipping I must use the only means available to me: my own urine. They would not think twice about a leaking latrine-can. I must hide the nail in between two bricks where it can be readily placed in a hurry but remain invisible to someone standing in the doorway. I must work in short, concentrated stints so as to be able to conceal my activities before visits by the guards. I must chip away not individual bricks but a complete section of brickwork so that even when I am able to remove it, it will stand in position. Will I possibly have the time? And the luck?

But all these methodical, if hasty conjectures I do not remember applying – not consciously at least. Perhaps, when your life is at stake, practical measures are implemented instinctively and automatically – since the cost of omitting them is so great. I only remember that I worked away feverishly with my nail. My universe – my existence – depended on that piece of rusty metal and that small patch of brick. My precautions for concealing my work must have been effective, for when the guards came, a first time, a second, they detected nothing. This went on – I cannot say how long. Scratching, chipping with the nail; interrupted by sessions with grey-hair and fat-cheeks. It was a race against time, and against my own dwindling physical resources. At any moment I might be the target for one of those fusillades that came from the courtyard. Or before I could finish my work I might lose the strength to continue. I might crack, before then, under interrogation. And yet, in fact, the merest chance of escape, the slenderest factor in my favour, renewed, double-fold, my power to resist and endure. I was carried along, despite all, on a wave of almost exalted emotion. I was not powerless. I had found a means of escape.

30

Tuesday. In the Tube today, a strange incident. The train stopped for a long time at Stockwell. Word got round that someone had been taken ill in one of the carriages; and, looking down the platform, we saw him: a short, chubby man with thin wisps of hair, being led away by a couple of porters. His jacket and tie were crumpled over one arm. His shirt was partly unbuttoned. His exposed chest glistened with sweat. And as they led him to the exit his face was reddened and contorted. He was crying like a child.

And the strange thing was the expression of everyone watching. Perhaps they felt shock, pity, curiosity. Perhaps they even felt a little bit afraid. But the dominant look on their faces was one of satisfaction, of relief, even of renewed strength.

31

. . . There was a strong temptation to hack away blindly at the gradually loosening brickwork, breaking it off in lumps. But this would have meant almost certain discovery. I somehow kept to my plan of removing a single, replaceable section. Since I was working in the dark I was constantly afraid that I might cut a hole too small for me to squeeze through, but my reckoning proved sound. Either that, or I had not realized how thin even a few days in Gestapo hands would make me.

At length, there came a moment unreal in its simplicity. I chipped away a final length of mortar. I felt the whole section loosen and wobble. I pushed gently at the bottom of the section and it fell forward on to my hands. My first feeling was, oddly, disappointment. No light flooded into my cell. I had already begun bitterly to conclude, from the lack of light visible through the cracks made as I worked, that, if my chute theory were correct, and ruling out, on the grounds of the incoming draught, that the outer wall was also blocked, then there must be, as in the case of my grandfather's house, some metal plate on the outer wall stopping the passage of daylight. But, after removing the section of brick, I expected to see at least some glimmer of brightness. I had not prepared myself for two simple things. Firstly, that when I 'broke through' it would be night. Secondly (so desperately did I cling to the comparison with my grandfather's cellar), that there could be something else blocking the entry of light other than a plate or hatch. Had I used the evidence of my senses I might have put two and two together.

Scarcely pausing, I thrust my head, and then my upper body into the opening. If light was not entering from outside, then fresh air certainly was, in abundance, together with the lavender fragrance I had already detected. I found myself – just as I had hoped – in a steeply inclining passage of rough brick. Crawling up it – I was, remember, quite naked – was painful. But these were the least of my pains at the Château Martine. At the point where, in order to get any further, my feet would have to leave the floor of the cell, my head bumped into something fibrous and yielding. It was the dense, woody undergrowth of a lavender bush.

A more careful soul might have hesitated at this point; might have crawled back into the cell, replaced the brickwork, sat down and formulated a detailed plan of escape. I did not. I had heard many escape stories while I was in France. The successful ones were either scrupulously worked out in advance or they were the result of sudden, hazardously seized opportunities. It was the ones in between which failed. I had neither the time nor the detailed knowledge of the Château and how it was guarded – nor the resources of self-discipline left – to make elaborate plans. It was night. I had made a hole in the wall. If I was spotted and shot in the Château grounds – well, doubtless I would have ended up shot anyway. My only precaution was to squirm back into the cell and daub my already quite filthy, scarred and bruise-covered body with dust. A nude escape had numerous drawbacks, the most immediate of which was easy detection.

I clambered back up the chute, listened carefully for several moments, then parted the thick stems of the lavender bush. My heart was throbbing with a strange thrill, a genuine, wild elation.

I knew I would emerge beneath the wall of the south wing of the Château. The front of the Château was to my right, the 'Watteau' garden to my left. I did not know precisely what lay immediately south of the Château but I resolved on making for the nearest cover in a direction half-left.

The lavender bush provided an excellent screened vantage-point. My eyes, free of the pitch-darkness of the cell, quickly penetrated the lesser darkness of the open air. There was a narrow border of shrubs, of which the lavender bush was an occupant, running along the base of the Château wall. Then a wide gravel path. Then an area about thirty yards square, which alarmed me first of all by seeming to be enclosed on three sides by a high wall. It contained a jumbled array of flowerbeds, low walls, paths and glass frames. I guessed this was the old kitchen garden of the Château. On the right was an open space occupied by two trucks and heaps of miscellaneous supplies, oil drums and so forth, under tarpaulins. No sign of my hosts. There was clearly an exit at either end of the gravel path, close to the Château wall, but these were dangerous routes. I looked along the walls of the kitchen garden. I spotted a doorway – whether it actually contained a door I could not see – on the left-hand wall, perfectly placed for the half-left, south-easterly line of escape I planned. If I could get to that doorway and pass through it, I ought to find myself in the gardens proper, with plenty of cover, and well clear of the rear of the Château.

I twisted my head round and looked up at the towering southern wall of the Château – like some piece of extraordinary stage scenery. No visible lights, search-lights or otherwise; stars veiled by patches of cloud. No noise. I was surprised by this. Perhaps it was later in the night than I imagined, or else, the centre of activity of the Château being the courtyard, the outer walls remained undisturbed. Looking before me again, I could see no sentry posts or machine-gun positions. The Château was not decked out like a prisoner-of-war camp with barbed-wire fencing. My captors must have relied on the internal security of the building – or on the fact that most of their charges were soon in too debilitated a condition to escape. It seemed inconceivable, nonethe-less, that the place was not patrolled by sentries who made complete circuits of the walls. I had glimpsed already, en route to interrogations, the sentries on the terrace at the rear of the Château and perhaps they made regular tours of the side-wings. At any rate, I could see no Germans at present and I could hear no tell-tale crunch of approaching boots on the gravel. A last thought made me delay no more. It was the thought of my cell door being opened and of my bare feet being visible through the hole in the wall; and, strangely, it was the thought not so much of how cruel discovery would be at this point, but of how ridiculous it would look.

I began to crawl half over and half through the lavender bush. These plants are tougher than you think, and this was not so straightforward. Another absurd position in which to be caught. But, having got my knees clear of the wall, I raised myself, dashed across the gravel path, fell on to all fours amongst the frames and herb-beds and, in a strange quadruped shuffle, reached the doorway in the wall. No alarms were raised. The darkened vegetable patches and fruit bushes in the kitchen garden and the fresh night air seemed to welcome me like conspiring friends. In those few yards I cut my bare feet on sharp stones. Moreover, that friendly night air (this was September, in hilly country) was chill on my unclothed flesh. I scarcely noticed these things at first – though they were to matter later.

The doorway in the wall contained no door. I waited, listened, peered cautiously through the entrance; heard, saw nothing. The scene the other side of the wall was black and indistinguishable because of the backdrop of trees. But these same trees would cover my escape. I stepped forward through the opening – and came all but face to face with a sentry.

One has miraculous good fortune, and then one has miserable bad luck. The section of wall – about ten yards of it – between my doorway and the Château proper must have been used by sentries patrolling the buildings as a convenient urinal. Even as I peered out a sentry must have been doing what even the most dutiful of sentries are now and then constrained to do. At the point when I emerged he finished and turned to his left.

He saw my unclad body, I saw his pale face, about five yards away from me.

Curious encounters take place in war-time. A naked Englishman meets an armed German with his hands on his fly-buttons. They should either fight or flee, but they do neither. For a frozen second they stare at each other in surprise and curiosity. I believe it was my nakedness that saved me. The expression on my German's face was an appalled, even an offended one. Had I been clothed, I am convinced he would have reached for his rifle at once. Perhaps there is something disarming about an enemy with no clothes on; or perhaps a man feels absurd levelling a gun with his flies undone.

At any rate, I had time to turn and run, and before the German could gather his wits and take aim I was already hidden by darkness. I had been spotted, nonetheless. The alarm would be given; and I had the narrowest of head-starts. Darkness was my chief ally. But it was also a hindrance to speedy flight. You must try yourself running naked through wooded or even semi-wooded country in the dark to realize how quickly one's feet become punctured and lacerated, one's whole body and face whipped and torn by boughs and brambles, and how at every pace one runs the risk of a violent fall over some unseen obstacle or down some hidden ditch. In a short space I was cut and bleeding and had no idea which way I was heading. I would have given anything for a pair of shoes. I had reached the boundary of the Château grounds and plunged into thick woods, but I had no means of preventing myself travelling unwittingly in a circle back towards my pursuers.

I experienced all the agonies of a hunted animal. And yet I remember that, in the first stages at least, I scarcely felt any physical pain. I even felt a strange rush of gratitude for these branches and thick tangles of foliage which, even as I pushed on, scratched and snared me. Since then I have come to believe – a blatant case of the pathetic fallacy, no doubt – that the woods and the trees are always on the side of the fugitive and the victim, never on the side of the oppressor.

I halted now and then to recover my breath and to listen out. I heard no noise of a chase; but I had no idea how much distance I had put between me and the Château. I could simply stop and hide the night in the woods.

It was unlikely that a search would discover me in this sort of country – it was even possible that the Germans, in their present general state of retreat, would fail to mount a search at all. But at any moment the yapping of blood-hounds might demolish this optimism. It was also plain to me that a naked man, in daylight, would not be hard to pick out. I had to find some clothes before dawn.

I formed a rough plan. Assuming that I was travelling in a generally south-easterly direction, I ought gradually to veer towards the south-west and hope to strike one of the small tributaries of the Doubs. This would be a means of shaking off pursuit by dogs. Then my aim must be, avoiding the roads, to find clothing somehow at one of the hamlets in the region of Combe-les-Dames. I could, of course, seek refuge in one of these villages, but I dismissed the idea. It was too close to the Château for comfort, I did not know any reliable hide-outs and, now the retreat was in full swing, this whole region was probably swarming with Germans. It was by hiding in an unfamiliar village that I had been caught before. I had more faith, once I was clad and shod, in keeping to the woods and the cover of the country and heading on towards the villages near Besançon where I knew I could find friends. Not the least of my considerations here – though it really counted for little in a distance of a few miles – was that in travelling south-west I would be travelling against the direction of the German retreat and, emotionally at least, towards deliverance. What I did not know at that time was that the Germans were already pulling out of Besançon and that the Americans were pushing across from the Ognon to secure the retreat-route along the Doubs.

And what I also did not know was the actual direction I had been moving in and how many hours of darkness remained to me. I had assumed dawn was not far off. It was in fact only midnight. I had also trusted that I was travelling south-east, whereas in fact I had already, unwittingly, veered – too far – south-west and was doing the very thing I feared – circling the Château at no great distance from it. I missed the Doubs tributary. I eventually came upon a village. But certain features of it, even dimly visible from the distance, told me it was Frécourt, a village scarcely two kilometres from the Château and the very first place the Germans would search.

But, believing daylight was imminent, I had little choice. I battered at the door of an outlying farmhouse. You may imagine the scene, which in retrospect has strong touches of the grotesque and the comic, though at the time such notions counted for very little. I was a naked man, filthy and blood-smeared, hammering at the door of complete strangers. I did not think of the reaction of the occupants. I was only concerned that they would not hand me over to the Germans. Some trace of civilized delicacy still clung to me in my primitive state and I tore a leafy branch from a bush for purposes of decency. I stood like Adam after the Fall.

The door was opened, warily, by a woman, in her forties, with an oil lamp, clutching the folds of her dressing-gown. Her eyes went wide as saucers.

There was no time for elaborate explanations:

'*Madame, je suis un agent Anglais. J'ai échappé aux Boches. Je vous en prie, donnez-moi des vêtements.*'

This was the first time, in addressing a stranger, that I had dispensed with my French 'cover'. I called myself an '*agent Anglais*'. I thought this would add to the effect.

My potential saviour stared at me for several seconds. She was interested less in my nakedness than in the filth and bloodstains that covered me. For a moment her face indicated nothing. Then she said, in the most collected of voices: '*Entrez monsieur. Attendez ici.*' And I knew I would be provided for.

She left me and returned in no time with a large blanket, towels and clothes; then went out again and reappeared with a bowl of warm water and a cloth. She beckoned me into a room and spread the blanket over a sturdy armchair.

'*Asseyez-vous. Lavez-vous et mettez ces vêtements.*'

I was touched by the way that in the midst of harbouring a fugitive ally she was concerned for her armchair.

She went to a sideboard, took out a bottle of wine and a tumbler.

'*Buvez. Je vais vous apporter quelque chose à manger.*'

It was only now as I began to bathe myself that I

realized how I had suffered in the course of my flight. My feet and ankles were raw, bloody, deeply gashed in several places and – for the first time – stabbingly painful. All this was on top of what had been wrought at the Château. A sense of having no time to spare, together with the pain involved, made me none too thorough about the washing. I slipped on the underwear and trousers I had been given. They were a shade too small.

The woman returned with soup, bread and cheese. Now that I was decently clad she allowed herself to inspect me more closely and to examine my wounds. She knelt and looked at my feet, uttered a brief exclamation of sympathy and began rinsing them gently. This hurt a great deal. '*Allez – mangez, buvez,*' she said. She spread towels under my feet so that the splashes of blood and filth would not touch the floor. It struck me that this was to avoid future evidence of my presence; but it must have already left incriminating footprints in the hallway. I realized the extreme risk she was running. She was a capable, dignified – and handsome woman, with reserves of warmth behind her alert grey eyes and disciplined, unpanicking features. Circumstances lend attraction to women – but this reflection is unfair to her.

I gulped at the wine. Though I had been starved for several days and my belly must have craved sustenance, I could not face the food.

'*Ces vêtements, madame. Ils sont à votre mari?*'

'*Oui. Les Boches l'ont tué. Il y a un an.*'

She left the room and returned with some thick socks and a pair of the sturdy leather boots beloved by the Maquisards and almost impossible, at this stage of the war, to get hold of. I had always preferred to be lighter shod myself, but I did not complain.

As I was pulling on these boots – like the clothes; they were a size too small and consequently, though they gave protection, they exacerbated the pain of my existing wounds – we heard the unmistakable noise of a German 'arrival'. Cars, the squeal of tyres, commands – the dreaded barking of dogs. The sounds came from the centre of the village.

We both stood up. Stabs of pain shot up my legs.

'I must go,' I said. I wanted to quash any attempt by this good woman to hide me. But she seemed already to have concluded for herself that I stood a better chance by flight.

I laced my boots. 'You must hide all this,' I said, pointing to the stained towels and blanket, the tray of uneaten food.

'Don't worry. They will know nothing.'

I believed her.

The sounds from the centre of the village were beginning to spread out. She went to a back window.

'Quickly.'

She ushered me to the door through which I had entered and opened it. She must have taken in the significance of the dogs (what presence of mind!) for she pointed to the right (the opposite direction to the one in which I had arrived) and said: 'Over there – there is a stream. Then after, the forest.'

I had no time to say more than *'Merci madame. Mille fois, merci.'* We embraced quickly, just as, in France, two men would have embraced in the same situation. Later, I reflected on this woman's extraordinary coolness and bravery – all without asking me questions. I was quite sure she would cope with the searching Germans. I did not know who she was and she did not know me. I promised myself that whenever it was possible I would return to thank her properly. But I confess, to my shame, I was never able to trace her.

I made off in the direction she had pointed out. I had ascertained from a clock in the house that the time was half past one. There were perhaps four hours of darkness left.

I crossed the little stream, slipping, almost disastrously, on a boulder, and made for the trees. I was now back in the mad world of flicking branches and clawing brambles, with my pursuers, this time, definitely on my trail. I was soon experiencing the paradox that rest, in the middle of great effort, can produce exhaustion. For a good twenty minutes, in the farmhouse, I had regained my breath, quenched my thirst, had my aches and wounds nursed, and the result of all this was not renewed energy but redoubled fatigue. Every movement was now becoming a distinct labour. On top of this, the boots I had squeezed into were beginning to make the already painful condition of my feet intolerable. At some point along the way I did a seemingly senseless thing. I took them off and threw them away (only an hour before I had been craving shoes), retaining only the woollen socks. I even debated whether to remove my borrowed clothing; for though, like the boots, they offered protection against the spears and barbs of the forest, they seemed, after several days of nakedness, a weighty encumbrance.

I was now, evidently, in a sorry state: making rash

decisions based on my immediate physical sensations without any degree of forethought. How would my unshod feet help me when I had to emerge into daylit streets? As I threw off the tight-fitting jacket, it did not occur to me that I was laying a convenient trail of divested garments for my pursuers. Rather, it seemed that, quite deliberately and actually – not as some metaphorical gesture – I was trying to turn myself into an anonymous creature of the woods. In this irrational idea hope seemed to lie. Perhaps I was delirious. Through all the agonies of my flight, I did not lose the sense that the trees, the leaf-strewn ground I trod were my friends. In fact, it grew. Amongst the pines and chestnuts there were sometimes small rustlings and scurryings. Owls hooted. Even as I blundered on, I thought: nocturnal animals are fleeing from me, just as I am fleeing my hunters. If only I could follow their example, disappear into holes and roots. Merge with the forest . . .

At some time after my departure from the village – a matter of hours or only moments, I do not know – I seemed to hear the noise of a stream behind me and of dogs crossing it and tracking along its banks. I had that sensation which sometimes comes in nightmares: that while you are straining every muscle to escape some pursuer, you are really making no ground at all; you remain helplessly in-motion-yet-stationary while your enemy closes. At another time I thought I heard, close behind me, German voices – the snapping voices familiar from the Château. I even thought I saw lights flashing at me through the trees. I don't know, now, whether I really saw or heard these things or whether they were hallucinations. Once, gunfire seemed to rip the air. When I stumbled and fell it took an age to get up. Then a time came when I could no longer remain on my feet and had to make the decision that the hunted rabbit or the cornered mouse has to make as the dogs draw in or the cat prepares to leap: to crouch, to huddle, offering no token of defence, waiting either to be pounced on and destroyed or for some miraculous intervention of destiny.

I made a hollow in the undergrowth, covering myself with leaves, and curled up in it. Some tall beech trees groaned in the wind above me. I was shivering, semi-delirious, hungry (I should have eaten when food was offered me), had lost my sense of direction and did not know where I was. I remember thinking, before drifting into merciful sleep, Yes, I am no better than some burrowing animal.

And destiny was to intervene, miraculously, in the form of the American Seventh Army . . .

32

On the way back from Quinn's I stopped by at a pub – a little pub on the edge of Wimbledon Common I haven't been to for some time. I got quite drunk, as if I were celebrating. But didn't I have something to celebrate? Gain. Loss. Sometimes they're the same thing. And whether it's for better or worse, there's something intoxicating, some-thing exhilarating about those moments which make you realize life won't ever be the same again. When I got back Marian said, 'How's Dad?' and I looked at her in astonish-ment. And then I remembered that, of course, Marian thought I'd been to see Dad. 'Haven't you been to see Dad?' she said. 'Yes, yes. Dad's fine,' I said. 'Fine, fine.' And then I said, 'I am going to be promoted. I am going to get Quinn's job.'

Quinn's house – or Quinn's ground-floor flat, for such it turned out to be – was somewhere in the leafy region between Richmond Park and Richmond proper. Perhaps you know this district of solid old villas set amidst their own miniature woodlands, and little urban cottages along narrow lanes which imitate the country. Through gates and bay-windows and the odd open front door, you catch glimpses of expensively and elegantly furnished interiors – decanters on sideboards, framed prints on the walls, gilt mirrors, that sort of thing. I don't like neighbourhoods of this sort. They smack of privilege and importance (you see how I betray my envy; the truth of the matter is these houses make me think of Dad and Mum's house in Wimbledon) and they smack, too, with their burglar-alarms and brick walls capped with broken glass, of distrust, of secrecy. And I don't like the way these civilized, urbane, well-pampered dwellings appropriate for themselves an air of the countryside as if they alone have a right to it. Because the trees, the leaves, they aren't really like that at all. They are there for everyone. But, again, perhaps this is envy speaking.

It took me some while to find Quinn's house – even though, in fact, it was not in one of the more secluded parts, but in a row not far from the main road. I admit, I was more than a little bit afraid. My heart was thumping, I was sweating. Were these the sort of surroundings, the sort of trappings that would be mine if I got Quinn's job?

But something helped to put me at ease almost immediately. The house in which Quinn lived was a tall, three-storeyed building at one end of a smart terrace. Dark brick; white portico; brass letter-box. Railings separated the front area from the pavement, and to reach the front door (solid, glossy black) you had to climb four or five steps. I thought: what would you expect from a man who even at his place of work has to be approached by a flight of stairs? I was half prepared to see Quinn's face at the front window, which was above street level, looking down at me as I got out of the car, just as he looked down at me, like a hawk, at the office. But all this was reversed as I passed through the front gate. For there, suddenly, was Quinn himself, standing not above me, but below me, in the little well around the basement window. He was wearing a loose, open-necked shirt, corduroy trousers and sandals, over socks, and was carrying a watering-can. One of his fingers was bandaged. I looked down at his sticky, bald forehead and the curls of grey hair visible where his shirt was open. He did not look like the boss of a police department but like some amiable, slightly dotty, retired professor.

'Ah, Prentis. Excuse me receiving you like this. But the flowers, you know, they have to be looked after.' There were pots of geraniums on the ledge of the basement window. 'No, don't go up to the front door – I seldom use it. This way.' He gestured to the steps down, then ushered me along the little path around the side of the basement. 'You look hot. Let me get you a drink.'

At the back of the building was a walled garden, with a lawn, roses, honeysuckle, two stunted apple trees and some rather rampant borders. Immediately to the rear of the basement, which was now on the level of the garden, was a small conservatory, opening onto a paved area on which there stood two wicker chairs and a fold-up table. I somehow expected all this. The conservatory was full of foliage. So Quinn was a lover of plants, too, a devotee of the flower-pot; like Marian. Through the conservatory was a large, sprawling kitchen, the result of more than one room knocked together – the sort of kitchen in which you can not only cook but eat, with several guests, and even lounge in like a living-room. From the cluttered, casual appearance of this room I got the impression that Quinn spent most of his time here. And, in fact, I never got to see the other rooms. I wanted to see all I could. For all the time, you see, I was looking for clues, for spy-holes into Quinn's elusive private life. I wanted to know, for example, whether there had been – still was – a Mrs Quinn; whether Quinn – somewhere – had sons or daughters. I never discovered these things. But I discovered enough.

Round the kitchen and conservatory roamed two (later I saw a third) Siamese cats.

'I'm going to have a gin with a big slosh of tonic and bags of ice. Will you join me?'

He beckoned me to sit down on one of the wicker chairs. While he busied himself inside at the fridge and the sink I noticed that in the conservatory, amongst a collection of various outdoor garments and implements – shoes, an old coat, a birch broom, walking-sticks – was a bag of golf-clubs.

He returned with two large, fizzing, clinking glasses.

'There's no need to behave as though we're at the office. Please, don't swelter in that jacket. Take your tie off.'

You see, I had dressed myself up smartly, like some boy applying for a job.

I took my glass. There were long bars of sunlight across the lawn; the fragrance of honeysuckle. I thought: where is the catch? As he gave me my drink I studied the bandage on the finger of his right hand.

We dipped our noses into our glasses and looked at the garden. Then Quinn spoke.

'So you came, my dear chap. You know, I had my doubts whether you would. No, not really, I was sure you would.' He took a hurried sip of gin – as if he had begun badly – then smacked his lips, and wiped his glasses which had become speckled with bubbles.

'Now. You have some questions you want answered. And I have some explaining to do. That's the position, isn't it?'

He gave me a penetrating but shifting look. It was as though he had said, 'You still want to go through with this?'

'Excuse me for using a cliché, but I don't know if this is going to be harder for me or for you. For me, it's a confession – of a kind. For you – well, you must make up your own mind. I'm saying this just as a way of telling you that if you find yourself wanting to cut the whole thing short, to forget the whole thing – though somehow I don't think you will – please, don't hesitate.'

As he spoke, one of the Siamese cats came and rubbed itself sinuously against his leg. Quinn put out his hand and fondled the scruff of its neck. He did this, not in a gentle, stroking way, but almost roughly, as if, at any moment, his hand might close round the animal's throat. Siamese cats, they say, are different from other cats. They don't ooze affection. There's something unpredictable, even sinister about them.

I shrugged awkwardly, as Quinn, still stroking the cat, seemed to wait for me to give some signal.

'You want to know what is going on at the office. But it doesn't stop with the office. That's the whole point. Our office isn't just an office, it spreads everywhere. Do stop me, Prentis, won't you, when I waffle? Well, shall I begin?'

He gave the cat a shove and it slunk broodily away.

'C9. And especially File E of C9. That is the particular point at issue, isn't it? But it's only an example of something general. You don't have to tell me, Prentis. You've been making private inquiries into C9, haven't you? I've half been egging you on to do that very thing. I know why you've been coming into work early and about – what shall I say? – your private correspondence with the Home Office. No, I'm not accusing you of anything – *I* should talk. I've been terribly undecided about all this. We'll get round to C9 in a moment – I'll put all the pieces together for you. But I can tell you now that I've had File E all along, and I nearly destroyed it. And it's not the only one. But shall we deal with the general matter first? That's what you said – you remember, when we spoke last – that you'd rather clear up the general issue first. Very well. I'm not going to say to you, Prentis, as I might, that I hope what I'm about to tell you will go no further and you'll keep quiet about it. Because, for one thing, it doesn't work like that. I'm not trying to defend myself. If you liked, you could put me through the mill. Don't look alarmed. And for another thing, I can trust you to make your own judgement. Yes, I'm asking you to judge me – because I, in my way, have been judging you. You've been aware of that, haven't you? And what I'm going to tell you is only an example of just the kind of judgement – am I being clear? – I'm asking you to make. I mean, how much you should tell, and how much you should keep silent, and how much you should know.'

The glow on the garden wall and the flowerbeds seemed to deepen almost perceptibly.

'Do you think there's enough trouble, enough misery in the world without causing any more?'

This came like a sudden challenge.

'Well – yes.'

'So you wouldn't condemn the action of someone who tried to eliminate extra misery where it could be avoided?'

'No – not on the face of it.'

'Thank you, Prentis. I've alluded to all this before, haven't I? That great heap of secrets at the office. A cupboard full of skeletons – I think that was the phrase I used. I wonder if I really have to spell it out to you. You must have worked out for yourself by now what I've been up to.'

I looked into my glass of gin.

'Well?'

I swallowed. 'You've been withholding – or destroying – information so as to spare people – needless painful knowledge.'

It was as though I had voiced something that had been pressing on my conscience for years.

'Precisely. I knew you would arrive at it. Do you know, I *wanted* you to arrive at it. To help me. And – what a benevolent construction you put upon it!'

I was looking at my hands. Somehow I didn't want to look at Quinn's face.

'You see, there are two types of power madness. No, no – don't dispute it – it's power we're talking about, and power mishandled. There's plain and simple corruption. We all know about that. Think of the harm, think of the sheer destruction you could wreak if you wanted to, if you were in my position.' I looked up at this point, and there was something sharp, almost like a mischievous gleam in his eyes as he said, catching my gaze, 'in my position'. 'We'd all agree that that's wrong, wouldn't we? But what about the opposite of that? What if you just as surely pervert your power and overstep the bounds of your responsibility under the notion that you are doing good? Is that wrong too?'

'I – I would – ' I looked away from Quinn again. I was experiencing the capsizing feeling that the very thing I sought most – Quinn's job – was the thing I wanted least. The old suspicion that Quinn was mad – and, in his shoes, I would be mad too. For a moment, I really wanted to be ignorant, an irresponsible underling.

'That's all right. What should I expect you to say? "Yes"? Or even "No"? I'm not here to ask questions anyway.'

'And what is the alternative,' he went on, 'the straight course, I mean? The straight course is to curb the imagination. To sit with all that knowledge and just to sort through it as if it had nothing to do with you. And that's why – if you have any imagination at all' (as he said this I faced him again and there was the same gleam in his eye, but no longer mischievous, almost sad) ' – the best, the securest position to be in is not to know. But once you do know, you can't do anything about it. You can't get rid of knowledge.'

I thought of Marian – Marian like a stranger in the same bed. All those nights seeking enlightenment.

'Do you know what the hell I'm talking about?' He gave a wry smile. 'I said it was madness. I'm not absolutely lunatic, mind you.'

One of the cats – perhaps the same one as before – drew near his seat again, and as it stood, uncertainly, about a yard away, he stared at it, then made a sudden jerking movement, as though to pounce on it, so that it gave a start and turned away. I thought: Quinn could be cruel to these cats.

'Do you know what makes you different from Fletcher, Clarke and O'Brien, Prentis? They're happily lacking in imagination . . .'

He toyed with his glass. For a long time he seemed to be bracing himself to speak.

'You can't get rid of knowledge. But I believed I could. At least, I believed I could get rid of knowledge on other people's behalf – before it became their knowledge. I used to sit at that desk of mine and think of all those people who – were within my power. I started to take files from the shelves. I started little inquiries of my own – from the reverse end. I started to destroy information. I used to think: here is such and such an individual – just a name in a file – who will now never have to know some ruinous piece of information. He'll never even know his benefactor. I used to think I was actually ridding the world of trouble. Good God. And the motive behind all this – was nothing but the desire for power.'

He paused for a moment, removed his glasses, wiped them. He looked, for the first time, in my eyes, like a man without any power at all.

'I warned you, Prentis. If you want me to stop, just say so.'

I shook my head.

'Very well.' He took a sip of his drink, replaced his glasses. 'The irony of it all – the absurdity of it all – was that in order to continue what I supposed was this benevolent scheme I had to put up a screen around myself so I wouldn't be found out; and, to keep people at a distance, I found myself having to behave the very opposite of benevolently. I'm afraid I've been a bit of a tyrant.'

'So, you mean – all your – '

'All my high-and-mighty bloody-mindedness?'

' – was just a cover? But you must have known that sooner or later the missing files and so on would have been discovered.'

'Yes, but I thought if I spread enough intimidation around nobody would dare do anything about it.'

'And the mixed-up files – the inquiries that didn't lead anywhere at all?'

'Red herrings – to cloud the issue. You see, I thought that if you or one of the others got wind of something, then the more generally confusing I made things, the better. The fact is, by this time, I was beginning to work hard at this other role – not just a cover – baffling people, making people afraid of me. Suspiciously hard. Did it work? A good performance?'

'It worked.'

An anxious, almost desperate look had come into his face.

'But only up to a point. Up to a point. Here, you'd better drink up, we're getting to the difficult part.'

We both drank. Everything in the garden was perfectly still. I thought of the patients on the terrace, with their tales of woe.

'Do you know at what point my little bid for power – my little enterprise for the good of mankind – broke down? Can you guess? It was all right, you see, doing good turns for people who were only names in files. I didn't have any qualms, then, that what I was doing was keeping from them the truth. I thought, they can do without the truth. But when it suddenly became a case of keeping the truth from someone I knew, then it was a different matter. I began to waver. Oh yes, I've always been a waverer – but

I *really* began to waver. What do you do? Let the truth out, always, no matter how painful? I began to get conscience-stricken. You know who the person is I'm talking about, don't you?'

I looked at him. His bald head shone. I had forgotten he was my boss.

'At first I thought there was an easy way out. When your father – became ill. When he ceased to speak. I thought, that puts a better seal on things than ever I could. It's all right, Prentis, I'll explain in a moment. No, but that was *too* easy. And it didn't solve the real issue. Supposing your father – forgive me – were to speak again. And the evidence, in any case, was still traceable. So I started to sound you out. I thought the only fair basis on which to proceed, either way, was your own disposition. I started to test you, to find out if you were the sort of person who would always want the truth – regardless of the cost – or not. I already knew about that fertile imagination of yours. I began to lay down little clues, little hints, to see how you would react. They must have become rather transparent in the last few weeks. And when you seemed to be cottoning on, I'd get scared and come down hard on you. I've been blowing hot and cold, I know. It's a funny thing, isn't it, how you start off wanting to protect someone and then, for that very reason, you end up torturing them? And as I was conducting this little test on you I began to realize that I was testing you for quite another reason too. I knew my retirement would be on the cards this year. Another way out of the problem, if you like. But it's not. I used to wonder, what will happen when I go? What will happen to my little half-baked scheme to save the world? All right – the sort of person they need in my job is the firm, inflexible – unimaginative type. But, between the two of us, I hope they never get him. You see, here I am, confessing away like a sinner, but the truth of the matter is – I'm going round in circles, I know – I'm not convinced that I've done wrong. Anyway, I put you to the test. And I found out firstly that you weren't the sort of person who would stop at finding out the truth – you *wanted* to know; and, secondly – I hope this doesn't shock you – I found out you were just a little bit like me. There were times when you almost came and had it out with me weren't there? – and then you didn't. You want your little bit of power as well, and you can't entirely control your actions, and – forgive me for speaking like this – you really want to be rather better than you are.'

So it was true. I had been spied on. I had been the subject of an investigation.

'What I'm saying – I'm not being clear, I'm sorry – is that ultimately I can't trust anything but my own instincts, and when I've left the department, I'd like to know that it's being run, well, shall I just say – wait till you've heard everything – by someone who will – trust his own instincts too.'

He turned to face me. Deep in his eyes again was that needle-like gleam.

'Shall we get down to particulars? How much have you found out – you know what I mean – about C9?'

I drew a long, shaky breath.

'That Z was a friend of my father's. That X may have been imprisoned by the Germans at the same time, and at the same place, as my father.'

'No more? Enough. Look I want to say at the beginning that what we're dealing with here isn't necessarily the one hundred per cent proven truth. I've been talking just now about the truth. It's hard enough withholding the truth when you're sure it's the truth you're withholding. But it's ten times worse when there's even the shadow of a doubt that it might not be the truth at all. All your pangs of conscience for nothing. But if it's a lie, Prentis, then maybe you have a right to know the lie as well. Now, do you want to know what was in File E?'

I nodded. My voice had gone.

'File E contained documents relating to X which came to light soon after X's death while undergoing trial. These documents contained evidence which might have been grounds for further investigation or even further criminal charges, but because X was dead the case was closed. The Home Office concluded their own investigations and were satisfied that both Y and Z were innocent victims of a malicious attack. Amongst the documents in File E – I can let you see them, I haven't destroyed them – yet – was a letter, or the copy of a letter, addressed to your father. Attached to this was another, long letter, clearly meant to be copied and circulated, since it was accompanied by a list of addresses. These included two newspapers, your father's publishers, a number of former members of special operations – and so on. There was another letter, addressed to Z, but I'll come to that later. The letters involving your father were the set-up for a blackmail. The gist of the blackmail was this: that your father did not escape from the Germans – from the Château Martine. He succumbed under interrogation, betrayed several resistance units and the whereabouts and covers of three British agents operating in the extreme east of France; and in return for this the Germans "allowed him to escape".'

I looked at the dead-still garden. Before me was the vision of a naked man fleeing through a dark forest.

'Do you want another drink? Let me tell you, Prentis, I've read your father's book – more than once. When it came out – before I met you. I've admired what's in it. Oh yes, I know I'm not the patriotic type, not the type to look for heroes. But I was around at the same time, I had my own little part in the war. And I can appreciate – this is the whole nub of it, Prentis – how a son might feel about such a father.'

Something had collapsed around me; so I couldn't help, in the middle of the ruins, this strange feeling of release. *I* had escaped; I was free.

'Can I see the file?'

'I'd wait a bit if I were you. Till we've talked it over. The letters put things rather more strongly than I do. They say your father was a coward and a traitor . . .'

'Were the letters sent?'

'No evidence of it. The ones to the publishers and so forth, definitely not – but they were the back-up letters to the initial one to your father. Your father never came forward. Of course – forgive me – blackmail victims often don't.'

'Were they dated?'

'No. The usual blackmailer's precaution. But obviously they must date from before X's death, and, as the back-up letters were never sent and as, to judge from the Y case, where Y was barely given time to make a pay-off before the allegations were made public (X tended to work fast, which supports the pure malice theory), they must date from a time shortly before X's committal for trial. That's to say, about two years ago.'

'Two years ago was when Dad had his breakdown.'

'Exactly. But don't jump to conclusions. There's no evidence for a connexion between the two things. And even supposing your father did receive the letter and his breakdown was a consequence, it may have been a reaction to a vicious, sudden, but still false allegation.'

'No – ' Suddenly, I don't know why, my voice became angry. 'Dad wouldn't have reacted like that. If it had been false, he would have faced it out, denied it, cleared himself.'

Why was I speaking like this? I thought: or, if he'd broken once, he would have broken twice.

'But, in any case,' – I faltered – 'maybe that doesn't matter. Maybe that's academic. There is still the fact of the allegation.'

'Yes. I'm afraid it's you who must bear the brunt of that. Your father may know nothing. At any rate – he's silent on the matter.'

The perfect defence: impenetrable silence.

I peered into Quinn's face – as if, now, he had become an easy target for me – for several seconds.

'Do you think it was true?'

Quinn threw up his hands. 'My dear chap, that's a question I can't answer.' His face looked pained. I thought: he is regretting he ever spoke – didn't keep silent too. 'I don't know if it can ever be answered. I've weighed up the known facts. You must do the same. X was a British agent in '44 and was a prisoner in the Château Martine at a time coinciding with, or close to the period of your father's imprisonment. All that is established fact.'

'So X would have known.'

'He would have been in a position to know. But he would also have been in a position, several years later, to make a spiteful, unfounded attack which had an apparent historical basis. Come back for a moment to the present and the other cases in C9. Y and Z were cleared: that itself speaks in your father's favour. All the evidence suggests that X was an embittered failure who wanted to get his own back on those who had fared better than himself. One of the charges he was up for before he died was *fraud*. Y and Z were successful civil servants on their way to the top. X's own civil service career was a flop. X was a British agent like your father, but he didn't come out of the war, like your father, a hero. The man felt neurotically inferior.'

Quinn turned in his chair and the little sharp gleam flashed in his eyes just for a second. I thought: if I had known what I know now, and the circumstances were different – I might have blackmailed Quinn.

'But if Dad did betray the other agents, isn't there evidence to corroborate that?'

Quinn bent forward in his chair and passed a hand over his face.

'In mid-September '44 three British agents were rounded up, almost simultaneously, by the Germans and shot, in Mulhouse. X mentions this in his letter – but it's a genuine fact.'

'So –'

'Wait. Don't forget there are two ways of looking at it. X wants to incriminate your father. He searches round for facts, coincidences, that will apparently do this. His whole purpose is to suggest the wrong sort of deduction.'

'But there are too many coincidences – X being at Château Martine, the shot spies, Dad's breakdown at the time the letter might have been sent –'

Quinn passed his hand over his face again. I thought:

he really believes Dad is guilty, but he is straining every nerve to protect me.

'Was he a traitor?' I blurted this out naïvely – as if Quinn were omniscient. The word 'traitor' sounded like something out of melodrama.

'Perhaps that isn't really the question. The question is, if he was, could you bear knowing it?'

I thought of the day when I refused to go any more with Dad to the golf course.

'There's one thing – that seems to go against all this. His book – '

'Ah – '

'The last pages, where he describes the Château, and his escape.'

'I've read them.'

'They're too convincing not to be real. He couldn't have written those things, if they never happened.'

'He knew the Château, and the region – and perhaps he had – like you – a strong imagination. If he wanted to invent an escape story he could have done so. I'm just pointing this out, not disagreeing with you.'

'No, I don't mean just that. The last chapters are *more* convincing than the other parts of the book, even though the other parts are about things nobody disputes are true. It's not just the authentic detail – it's the tone.' I felt my voice running away with me. 'In the rest of the book you hardly sense Dad's feelings, you don't sense Dad himself. But in the last paragraphs you – '

I looked at the pale, peppery hairs, visible on Quinn's chest.

>   . . . of all the humiliations . . . none was more demoralizing, more appalling . . .

'If he didn't actually escape, if it was all a deal with the Germans – why should he write a false story anyway? Why should he have written his book at all and put himself at risk. Shouldn't he have just kept quiet?'

'Because he had to justify how he got out of the Château. He couldn't just say, They let me go. His war record up till then had been pretty remarkable – the grand finale had to live up to it. Of course, I'm speaking hypothetically. But to continue the hypothesis. Suppose that this brilliant record really was blotted by a final act of betrayal; suppose that his hero's reputation rested ultimately upon a lie. Imagine the pressure, the burden of this – the fear of the truth coming out. Have you ever wondered why it was so long after the war before your father's book appeared? 1957. He was approached before then by more than one publisher. Why? Because he hesitated over the final act of committing the lie to print, of becoming an out-and-out impostor. At least, he hesitated up to a point. But then the mental pressure becomes too much. He starts to see the publication of his memoirs in a quite different light – as a means of rebutting once and for all the possibility of exposure, of presenting the hero-image in such a complete and thorough way that no one will dare challenge it. And think for a moment what happens when he actually does this. Why are the final chapters more convincing, more heartfelt than the rest? Because it's here the real issue lies. The *true* exploits, all the brave and daring deeds, what do they matter? They can be treated almost like fiction, but the part of the book that's really a lie – that's where all the urgency is. It's here that he's trying to save himself. Why does it read like a real escape? Because it *is* an escape, a quite real escape, of a kind. Who knows if in writing it your father didn't convince *himself* it was true? And why is it also the most thoughtful, the most sensitive, the most imaginative part of the book? Am I seeing too much in it? Because in writing it he is actually torn between the desire to construct this saving lie and an instinct not to falsify himself completely – to be, somehow, honest. So behind all the "authentication" of his prison experiences and of the escape, he puts down little hints, little clues, meant perhaps only for those nearest to him – for his own son – ' Quinn grew excited ' – clues which say, in case they should ever inquire beyond the surface: See, I was only human. I had my limits, my failings.'

Through the open door, that summer night, Dad's sudden start – as if I'd caught him in some guilty act.

I thought: who has the lurid imagination now?

'My dear fellow – I'm sorry, I didn't mean to say all this. I got carried away. Please – '

For a long time there was silence. I sensed Quinn's apprehension. Then suddenly I said, 'Did he break down?' My voice was savage. 'In the Château – did he break down?'

'My dear chap – '

'In the prison chapter, Dad is silent about what they did to him. He keeps saying: this can't be described, this is blurred.'

'Yes, but that would be quite understandable. He was tortured – that's almost certain – probably severely tortured – you must have considered that. You can't blame him for not dwelling on those things.'

The garden glimmered in the evening light. A mirage.

'Or,' I said, 'for quite naturally breaking down under them.'

He looked at me. He seemed suddenly perturbed, daunted by the vehemence in my voice. I realized I was defending Dad – defending that dignified dummy on a hospital bench.

Quinn said: 'Consider the possibilities. The Americans were advancing. He must have known the chances of being freed very soon: an argument for "holding out" – an argument against betrayal – and for not undertaking, if we're speaking now of the genuine article, a risky escape. On the other hand, the Germans were desperate. They were in retreat. They needed information, or they were simply extra-brutal' – his eyes sharpened – 'as desperate men are. Reasons for "breaking down" – or for effecting an escape even with liberation imminent.'

'But if the Germans were desperate what would have been the advantage of a betrayal? They might have shot him anyway.'

'True. But consider another possibility. He turns traitor – oh, scarcely with any object in mind, but simply because – like everyone – he has – a breaking point. Then he realizes the Germans will shoot him anyway – so he has to escape in earnest.'

He sighed. 'Will you have another drink?'

'No.'

He looked into his own glass and jogged the sliver of lemon at the bottom of it.

'I know what you're thinking. You hate me because I'm imparting all this information. Because I have the information – the file – I'm responsible for the fact. That's not logical. But I don't blame you. It's just the same at the office. Because you handle all that information, you feel to blame for it. You don't mind if I have another one, do you?'

He eased himself out of his seat, gripping his glass. 'You

see,' he suddenly said, 'this business of betrayal, and this business of breaking down – they aren't the same thing at all, are they?'

I watched him waddle to the kitchen through the conservatory. I had never seen him before out of his grey or dark-blue office suit. Like all professional men suddenly seen in casual clothes, he looked vaguely clownish and defenceless. The Siamese cats followed him at a distance. Shadows crept up the garden wall and up the branches of the apple trees.

... to make the decision the hunted rabbit or the cornered mouse has to make ...

Quinn returned. ' "Betrayal" sounds like some deliberate, some conscious act. But "breaking down" ...' He sipped his drink and smiled, gently, at me. 'Are we putting your father on trial or aren't we? Think of his predicament again. Alone in that cell, he has all those possibilities to weigh up. Nothing is certain, nothing is clear. If he doesn't "speak", the Germans will shoot him. If he does, will they shoot him anyway? Will the Americans arrive in time or not? Should he risk escape or risk waiting for liberation? If he speaks will it make any difference, at that stage, to the course of the war? Is a betrayal a betrayal if, in fact, it has no consequences? And then, on the other hand, if he *doesn't* betray, that may make a very real difference – between his own life and death. He has all this mental anguish, on top of confinement and – torture. And against all this he can only oppose one feeble imperative – his duty. It's a mystery; I don't know what really happened. But you can be sure of one thing. If he did betray, he only did what any ordinary, natural human being would have done – he saved his own skin.'

Quinn held his gaze on me and I looked away. The smile

had melted from his face and I felt he was studying me as he often did in the office, searching for reactions.

'Have I ever told you how I got my limp?' he said.

I looked at him, surprised.

He bent down suddenly and rapped the front part of his right foot with his knuckle. It gave a hard, hollow sound.

'You see, that part's not me.'

I looked, perplexed, and slightly repelled. I'd never known Quinn had an artificial foot.

'You're wondering what this has got to do with it? Let me tell you the story. It's not irrelevant. I was twenty-five when the war started, Prentis. Older than a lot of them. In '44 I was thirty – nearer your age – a junior officer who'd spent the war in camps and depots and hadn't heard an angry shot. I didn't have any lust for battle, you understand, but the fact rather irked me. Our battalion went over to Normandy. Not one of the first wave. It was ironic. There were men under my command who'd been in Italy and North Africa and I was supposed to lead them into action – and it was all rather important to me. We didn't see any fighting until we got to Caen – '

'Caen?'

'Yes, I know, your father was in Caen. You see – he was preparing the way for the likes of me. Well, I saw my bit of action, and it was all over in about a minute. I had to take my platoon across open ground towards a wood which, in theory, should have been flattened by our artillery. The Germans were there; they opened up, and in ten seconds half my platoon was dead. That's an astonishing thing when it happens, Prentis, believe me. I didn't perform any of my much-rehearsed functions as a leader. I obeyed my instinct. I ran like bloody hell – like everybody else. I ran *for my life*.

That's no joke. I would have killed any English soldier who got in my way, let alone a German. Now I don't remember any of this except one thing – it's perfectly true, memories *do* get blurred. As I ran I had to jump over a bit of broken-down hedge. Lying face up in the ditch on the other side of it was a wounded man. I don't know if I saw him beforehand or if I only realized he was there when I'd already jumped. All I know is that my right boot came down hard and firm on his face; and I had a good glimpse of his face because I was able to tell the poor fellow was still alive. I didn't stop. A few seconds later something knocked me into the air and the next thing I knew I was in the dressing-station. I'd lost half a foot and, fortunately perhaps, I wouldn't be called on to command any troops again; and the fact that I was wounded somehow obscured the possibility of my being charged for cowardice and dereliction of duty. You see if someone had accused *me* of cowardice, of betrayal, they'd have been perfectly right – but all that got lost in the confusion of battle. Now, I'm not necessarily superstitious, Prentis, but I can't help believing my right foot was blown off because it was that foot that trod on that man's face. Or is that just some guilty need of mine for punishment? But why punishment? Aren't there certain situations when the pressure of events is so intense, so overpowering – that even the most wretched action can be forgiven?'

I looked at him, puckering up my face.

He nodded. 'But that's not all. There's one thing I've never told anyone about that moment. When I brought my foot down – it was only a split second, but I remember this much – I thought: he's had it, I can still save myself. I was glad.'

I turned my eyes to the garden. As the shadows crept

upwards, they made the remaining chequers of sunlight, on the walls, the roses, the apple trees, more intense and dazzling. A sweet smell came from the honeysuckle. I remembered our garden in Wimbledon. Mother's kitchen garden. Her clump of lavender.

The smell of apple wood is the smell of sanctuary . . .

I thought: I'd wanted Dad to come back to me. Perhaps now I had the words – the question – that would shock him out of his silence. I could say to him: Did you betray your comrades? And his eyes would start into life. But at what cost to him? Was that the price of having Dad back? That he must know that I knew he wasn't a hero. And *did* I know that? If I found out myself – if I looked at the files and followed them up (how could I tell that Quinn wasn't still holding back some clinching piece of evidence?) – then I would know; but the world need never know. We could destroy the files. Was that what Quinn was offering me?

And in that case Dad must remain a silent statue.

I thought: if I knew that Dad hadn't been strong and brave, then I wouldn't hit Marian and shout at the kids and sulk around the house. But I didn't want to know that Dad wasn't strong and brave.

Quinn said: 'What are you thinking about?'

I'd never have guessed Quinn had no foot. He was patched up with metal, like the Bionic Man.

I said: 'I was thinking about my hamster. Do you know, for the last couple of months I've kept thinking about my hamster?'

He looked at me, wide-eyed. 'Will you have that other drink now?'

'Please.'

He got up. While he was indoors one of the cats drew near. I put my hand out to stroke it, but it backed away.

When he returned I said: 'You haven't told me what was in the letter to Z.'

'That's true.' He sighed. 'I've been saving it. Go back for a moment to what I said at the beginning. If you want to call a halt to this little discussion, just say so, whenever you like. Are you sure you want to know what was in the letter to Z?'

'Yes. I want to know everything.'

'All right. X's letter to Z was not, strictly speaking, a blackmail letter, since there was no accompanying demand. Though I suppose it might have been turned to that end later. It supports, again, the theory that X's allegations were purely malicious. The substance of the allegation was that your father had been having an affair with Z's wife. At the time of the letter this had been going on – so the claim was – for nearly a year.'

'But that can't be true.'

Quinn eyed me abruptly. I had not denied the other charges against Dad so hotly. All the strength of my denial was based on my memory of Dad and Mum.

'It needn't be true. Once again we're dealing with some-thing that, quite possibly, was wholly trumped up. But let me – since you want to know everything – put the opposite case. Z committed suicide at a time soon after he may have come into possession of this letter. No other motive for the suicide was revealed other than his wife's statements about their ruined marriage. That presumably had been a source of distress for some time, so it doesn't necessarily explain why Z took his life when he did. But supposing he suddenly gets knowledge of his wife's infidelity. That might have been the last straw, that might have brought him – why do we keep using this phrase? – to the breaking point. And not just his wife's infidelity. Z was a friend of your father – your own researches turned that up – a long-standing, close friend. He admired your father, respected him enormously. Compare their war records – doubtless you tracked this down too. Your father was all the things Z never quite became himself. You see, though Z became professionally successful, we're dealing with another man who was perhaps dissatisfied with his achievements, who perhaps had a nagging sense of inadequacy. What was intolerable about X's letter – if we assume he took it seriously – was not just his wife's behaviour but the fact that a friend he looked up to – even idolized, who knows? – had cheated him, and probably knew, what's more, via his wife, all his own pathetic circumstances – assuming *those* to be true – as a husband. A stronger man might have had it out with your father. What's a strong man? Z just collapsed. All this doesn't conflict with the wife's evidence. If her marriage to Z was really as she described it, she would have been ripe for an affair with another man. And, of course, she would have pushed the evidence she did give for all its worth – so as to hide the fact of her infidelity. Then there's Z's son. Remember, I told you that he turned against his mother after the inquiry. Might that not have been because he knew all about his mother's affair? He hated her both for her original unfaithfulness and then for dragging his father's name cold-bloodedly through the dirt.'

I thought: whose side is Quinn on? What does he want?

'And one other thing corroborates X's letter. To do with the dates. Nearly a year – '

'You mean – I know what you are going to say – it dates everything from shortly after my mother died.'

I thought of Dad's coldness to Marian.

'Yes. It would be another factor to support X's allegation. But, also – if we suppose that allegation wasn't false – something to mitigate your father's action. A man who loses his wife, quite without warning, still in his middle years. Grief; loneliness. He turns to another woman for some kind of solace. Oh, he's not absolved, by any means. But isn't he doing, again, what any ordinary man, with only so much strength, might do?'

I'd never wanted any other woman than Marian; only to be closer to Marian.

I turned my face again from Quinn because my eyes were smarting.

'I'm sorry. I've put everything in the most unfavourable light. You wanted me to tell you. If you wanted me to tell you, there seemed no point in softening the implications. You must think I'm a bit of a bastard. But, remember, all this can just as well be explained as an invention of X's spite. As a matter of fact, X's own marital history isn't irrelevant. Yes, he was married. Children. He was divorced about five years ago and about a year before his dismissal from the Home Office. His wife brought the petition. The grounds were cruelty.'

'Cruelty? Was the business of Z's wife mentioned, too, in X's letter to Dad?'

'Yes. X threatened to make it public.'

I thought: the subject of all this is sitting in a chair on a hospital terrace. I would be with him, normally, on a Wednesday. Is he waiting for me, missing me? Or is he none the wiser?

I looked at the lit-up garden walls.

My universe ... depended on that piece of rusty metal ...

Quinn sipped his drink. 'I know what you are thinking. You are wondering what happens now. I can show you the file, the actual letters. You can follow up the threads – as you have done already. You can find out if X was really telling the truth. Real police-work. Is that what you want? Perhaps you want' – he paused and narrowed his eyes – 'to destroy your father. But why should you want to do that? Isn't he – I shouldn't say this – destroyed already?'

'Which proves everything!' I said in sudden rage. 'His breakdown – at the time when it happened – is the one thing that clinches it all.'

'No, no, no. It doesn't clinch the *truth* of anything. Remember what I said. A breakdown can be triggered by a false accusation, by the *threat* of blackmail, as well as by the real thing. And in any case, supposing the letter did contain the truth and it did cause the breakdown – hasn't he effectively put the seal on the matter? Hasn't he rendered himself immune? And isn't he giving us a signal? I want silence on this business. I don't want to be approached. I want to be left alone with my knowledge. You see, it's the knowledge that matters, it's the knowledge that makes the difference. Only that. But let's get back to my point. You can follow the matter up – face it out with your Dad. Perhaps that matters to you. Or perhaps what matters to you is to preserve your father, to preserve the father who is in that book of his. Is that the case? Well, there is no reason why it shouldn't be. All of this perhaps can make no difference, externally; it can matter to no one except you. If nothing happens, the secret – the mystery, if you like – remains only with you, and me. Perhaps uncertainty is always better than either certainty or ignorance. Do you know what I propose? I propose destroying File E. Yes, our job is the *preserving* of information. Well, you'll have to shoulder that one when I leave the office – a small burden, perhaps, in the circumstances. The file's here, in the flat. Yes, another rule broken. It's up to you whether we destroy it, now. And it's up to you whether you want to look at it before it's destroyed.'

I met Quinn's eyes. I felt like a criminal.

'What about other people? People still alive—'

'There's always that risk of course. But then all this has slept for thirty years. Why shouldn't it go on sleeping? Your only real danger is Z's wife and Z's son. But Z's wife is hardly likely to want to publicize matters further, and Z's son – well, Z's son's primary concern was his father's reputation. Now his father has been cleared of any professional slur, he is hardly likely to want to make known – that's if my theory about Z's son is correct – that his father committed suicide because he had found out his best friend was carrying on with his wife. All these skeletons, Prentis, hidden away in cupboards. As a matter of fact, your position and Z's son's are peculiarly alike. You both want to protect your fathers. You are both under your father's shadows. Am I right? You never know, perhaps one day you should meet.'

Z's son. So, somewhere else in the world, there was someone like me.

'Shall I get the file?'

'All right.'

He went in once more. I sat with my drink, looking at Quinn's trim, new-mown lawn. I thought: this is just another terrace where you sit and play games with the truth.

He emerged with the file in his hand. It was a standard, pale-blue office file with the letters C9/E on it and 'CONFIDENTIAL' stamped in purple ink on one corner. He placed it on the table in front of me. I felt like a witness in the dock confronted with some incriminating exhibit.

'Now – first question. Down at the end of the garden is a little incinerator I use for burning garden rubbish. I suggest we have a bonfire. Do you agree?'

I looked at the file. For a while I didn't think of Dad at all; only of the implications of destroying official information.

'Yes,' I said.

'Good. If we don't decide now we might dither for ever. Second question: do you want to look at it first, before you even answer question one?'

I stared again at the file. I thought of the number of times I'd opened the cover of *Shuttlecock* hoping Dad would come out; hoping to hear his voice. Was I afraid that the allegations might be true – or that they might be false? And supposing, in some extraordinary way, that everything Quinn told me was concocted, was an elaborate hoax – if I never looked in the file, I would never know. I read the code letters over and over again. C9/E . . . And then suddenly I knew I wanted to be uncertain, I wanted to be in the dark.

'No,' I said.

'Right. Come on.'

Quinn got hastily out of his seat and took the file. He was like a boy engineering some mischievous prank. Was he doing all this simply to pass the responsibility on to me? I followed him across the lawn. I thought of him running in the fields of Normandy. We reached an unkempt corner of the garden, beyond the screen of the apple trees. Ivy cloaked the walls, and some neglected trees in a neighbour's garden arched overhead. Bits of garden debris and cinders strewed the ground, in amongst patches of weeds and nettles. It wasn't the safest place to have a fire.

The incinerator stood in the corner – a shaky, wire-mesh construction, rusty and scorched. Quinn stooped over it. He did not pause. He took a cigarette lighter from his trouser pocket and then dropped the file into the wire frame, lifting his arm, ritualistically, high. He turned to me for final confirmation.

'I've done all this for you, Prentis, but also to put my own mind at rest. If you think I was wrong, tell me.'

'I don't know,' I said, resolutely. It seemed to me this was an answer I would give, boldly, over and over again for the rest of my life.

Quinn looked at me, surprised, approving.

'Are we ready then?'

He flicked alight the cigarette lighter. Before setting the flame to the file he pulled out some of the documents and spread them loosely to help them burn. The papers blackened, curled and flared up. I thought of funeral pyres. I thought: they can arrest us for this.

I'm not superstitious, but I wondered if at this moment, as the flames licked at File E, Dad would be feeling, at the hospital, a glow of relief; whether others there would see his face brighten – his lips flutter. The smoke curled up through the overhanging leaves. The evening shadows had lengthened and the branches and foliage seemed to press round us in complicity.

... the woods and the trees are always on the side of the fugitive ...

Quinn crouched by the incinerator, poking the fire with a stick. The flames lit his face. He might have been an outlaw in some forest hideout.

'There,' he said, lifting the last fragments of paper to make them catch. 'Now it's done.'

'And all this was for me?' I asked. 'All those mixed-up files; your – behaviour – at the office? And you might never have told me about it?'

'Not exactly, old chap. There are others like you.' He smiled rather sourly. 'My little flock. I just happened to *know* you.'

I thought: do I really understand Quinn any better? You penetrate one mystery only to find another. I wondered if at work tomorrow he would behave just as before, as if this evening hadn't happened. Speak to me gruffly; look down at me from his glass panel; treat me like dirt. I looked at him as he crouched. His eyes were hidden by the reflected flames in his glasses. I remembered my arrival when he stood at the foot of the basement steps and everything was different. I felt vaguely as if I were under hypnosis.

'Well, shall we finish those drinks?'

He got up and tossed away the stick he was holding. As he did so he struck his hand – the hand with the bandaged finger – against the rim of the incinerator. He winced and clutched the injured finger. 'The cats,' he explained. 'Little beasts. They quite often bite me. Do you like Siamese, Prentis? Just a little bit on the wild side, a little bit devious – you won't ever show them you're the boss. I think that's why I've got them.' A sly look entered his eye. 'You see, I like animals, but I'm not sure I believe in keeping pets. Don't you think if you keep pets they should be free to rebel whenever they like?' He waved the bandaged finger. 'Come to think of it, they'll be wanting their supper now.'

We walked back across the lawn. I watched Quinn's limp.

The cats were prowling round the door of the conservatory. When Quinn went in they followed him.

He reappeared after a minute or so with a large bowl of cat-food and another of milk which he put down on the edge of the lawn. The cats began lapping and nibbling at once. Quinn squatted amongst them and stroked the neck of one of them as it ate. It twisted and rubbed its head against Quinn's hand, but whether out of pleasure or annoyance I could not say.

'By the way, you'll be getting official notice of your promotion tomorrow. Starting from when I leave, of course.'

He said this as if it were something merely minor and incidental but at the same time logical and expected. And, at first at least – until I had left Quinn's and was returning home – this was just how I received it. I nodded, smiled. So much else had happened.

I stayed only another five or ten minutes. We finished our drinks, the cats licking and preening themselves at our feet. Most of the time we talked about animals and pets, and, almost as a natural course, about children.

He walked with me to the front of the house to see me off. At the foot of the basement steps he said – and not at all in a voice that carried any of the double meanings and undertones the words might have had in the context – 'I do hope your father's condition improves'; and he extended his hand, to grip my own or perhaps to grasp my shoulder. But I had already begun to mount the steps, and when I turned at the top I saw him standing at the bottom, his right hand dropping awkwardly to his side. This was the last image I took away of Quinn. I say 'last' as if I never saw him again – which isn't true. But I have never seen again the figure in sandals and baggy, opened shirt, the figure with his watering-can and Siamese cats, or the figure who ran, to save his skin, in Normandy. For most of the time, you never know the real person. And then there was something about the sight of Quinn, standing, alone, on the front path as I started the car and waved to him from the window, that made me think: he looks like a man you will never see again.

I drove back scarcely conscious of my route. I should have been thinking of Dad, of X and Z, of *Shuttlecock*, of those three agents who were shot in Mulhouse ... And then suddenly – as if I really had been hypnotized and the hypnotist's fingers had been snapped before my eyes – the reality of Quinn's words struck me: I was going to be promoted – officially; I was going to get Quinn's job. And I had this sudden urge to get drunk.

I stopped off at the pub I knew, by Wimbledon Common. I was already tipsy from the gins I'd drunk. I hadn't eaten all evening and it was by now past the time when, had I been to see Dad as usual, I would have returned home for the supper Marian kept for me. But I stopped at the pub, ordered a large gin and tonic and took it outside to drink. People were sitting at wooden tables, chatting and laughing. It seemed I'd emerged out of some confinement. Perhaps the people were happy because of the warm summer twilight wrapping round them and making the world grow soft and dim. Perhaps it was all a case of the pathetic fallacy. Then I thought: these people are happy because of what they don't know.

When I got home Marian said: 'You're drunk.' (I'd had more than one drink at that pub.) 'You're drunk. You're late, and your dinner's spoilt.' It was like a scene in some hackneyed domestic comedy. I could see in her face her worry about where I had got to; and I could see that she thought the moment gave her a right to wield a little authority over me, to scold me, to have the upper hand. But I could see too that, despite her efforts, she was afraid to do this. She was afraid because I was drunk (I'm not often drunk, as a rule; I'm not a man who goes in much for big drinking) and because I was drunk I might hit her. (Though I won't hit Marian again, no, never.) But she was afraid, in any case, that if she attempted to scold me I would make her suffer for it. I could see this fear and this desire to have a little power struggling in her face and so I hugged her, kissed her and said, 'It's all right.' She was so surprised at this (it's a long time since I've given Marian a hug on my return home) that she became subdued, even wary. Her blue-green eyes flickered. 'How's Dad?' she said. Then I realized what she might be thinking: Dad's recovered, Dad's spoken again. That's why I've gone and got drunk. I thought: in a way that's just what's happened. She looked suddenly alarmed. And so I kissed her again. 'Dad's fine,' I said, 'fine, fine.' And then I said: 'I'm going to be promoted. I'm going to get Quinn's job.'

33

It is over six months now since Quinn left our office. His departure was marked by the minimum of ceremony. A gathering of senior staff in one of the offices upstairs, to which, of course, myself, Vic, Eric, Fletcher and O'Brien and most of our junior ancillary staff were duly invited. Drinks and little sausages on sticks. The presentation of a gift for which I took the initiative for collecting contributions, and which for some time remained a problem until I remembered the battered golf bag I'd seen in Quinn's conservatory. Golf-clubs are not cheap, and I don't mind saying that I myself forked out in secret an extra large donation in order to buy the set, complete with bag, that the man in the sports shop assured me was the best. Speeches. A short valediction in which Quinn kept strictly within the emotional limits prescribed by such occasions, not allowing any undue warmth to melt, at the last moment, his traditionally chilly manner; and in which he wished, with no hint of special sentiment, 'every success to my young and able successor' in the seat which was 'by now' (dutiful ripple of amusement) 'nicely warmed'. A breaking-up into general drinking, chit-chat and hypocritical well-wishing from which Quinn himself slipped away, scarcely noticed, not deigning to join us in the session which followed in the pub around the corner. I too slipped away from this second bout of drinking while it was still in its early stages, to learn later, from Vic, that it had developed into an orgy of Quinn-bashing, and from Eric – with whom, being now his superior, I found I could not listen to such things without making vague signs that he was being over-familiar – that this same session had led to another in which he had positively and completely explored all the remaining hidden charms of the tantalizing Maureen.

And so to the next Monday morning, and to sitting in that leather chair, which was not warm but distinctly cool (October; the office heating not yet coaxed into life), and which seemed, and still seems, I might add, too big for me.

I haven't seen or heard of Quinn since. No phone calls or invitations. No chance, passing visits back to his old office. I imagine that is how he wishes it to be. We will cease to associate, like old accomplices who have done the deed and gone to ground. Our mutual silence will be as constant as Dad's.

But very often, I think of Quinn. I wonder what he is doing; how he is spending his 'retirement'. For with a man like Quinn, so solitary, so formerly work-bound, there seems no way in which this phrase can conjure up its usual stock of clichés. What will he do? The only picture I can summon of him is of a man walking – no, limping – almost continuously over the turf of a golf course, dragging a bag of golf-clubs which have already lost their new shine, pitting himself, not against the skill of others (for some-how I am sure that Quinn, with his metal foot, is neither a good nor a competitive player), but against his own deficiencies, his own nagging uncertainties, harrying the little ball towards its far-off home. Or I see him, an even more solitary figure, on one of those mythical sea-cruises the newly retired are supposed to take, gazing from the stern-rail as the sun sets, over Madeira or Tenerife, and yet unable to drink in fully, to be pacified completely by the magic of the scene, because he cannot, ever, quite shake from his mind the memory of all those skeletons locked away in cupboards. I think, one day Quinn and I will meet, like secret agents at some seemingly innocent rendez-vous – to feed the ducks on Clapham Common, to watch the animals at the zoo. I think of Quinn when I go to see Dad. Quinn . . . Dad. One day they, too, must meet . . . But all these things, of course, are romantic visions. Lurid imagination. I think again. Quinn has his garden, his conservatory, his Siamese cats . . .

And I am left only with the after-image of Quinn's official self which I wear about my own person by virtue of occupying his desk. I look at the cherry tree through the window (nearly May again; it has passed the peak of its bloom). I summon Miss Reynolds (at first a shy and reluctant servant to a new, young master) on the intercom. I write down instructions. I survey the others (my old place taken by Eric) through the glass partition. I even suspect that I am developing the hint of a limp, and that one day, not far off perhaps, my hair will start to recede and I will simultaneously find myself in need of glasses.

And, what is more, I have the combination to the safe

that, previously, was accessible only to Quinn, and I have the right to unseal all those sealed files which, previously, only Quinn could open.

Eric has just looked up. He has seen me standing at the partition, sipping the cup of tea Miss Reynolds has brought me, and his eyes have betrayed that faltering compromise that I know so well from experience: not turning away at once, but hesitating to give the full counter-stare. A tense, awkward look, perhaps lasting two seconds. Then he lowers his head abruptly, with an air of returning purposefully to his work; and then, after a few seconds more, his hand goes up to push the hair from his forehead and scratch his crown – perhaps to give an added impression of industry, but more likely to signal to me in some pleading way (for he knows I am still watching) that he is puzzled. In the last few months this bewildered, anxious, even melancholy expression has crept into the features of Eric, who was never one, in the past, to let the business of the office unduly preoccupy him. Where is the Eric who once boasted of his conquests in the typing pool, and who did not let his wife and family stand in the way of his not entirely plausible adventures with Maureen (of whom he no longer speaks)? A reasonable deduction might be that added responsibility has sobered and per-plexed him; that in moving up the ladder from junior assistant number two to junior assistant number one (no huge advancement) he has come up against his own unhappy limitations. But I know this is not the case. He has every reason to be puzzled. Half the items in that file he is looking at now are missing.

I continue gazing at Eric, sipping my tea, knowing what my next move will shortly be. When my tea is finished I will open the rear door of my office and call out, like some captain on the quarter-deck, 'Eric – can you spare a moment?' (For, unlike Quinn, I cannot run – not with Eric, at least – to the barking of full-blown orders. But my words are a command – and a provocation – nonetheless.) And Eric will step up, and I will see the apprehension on his face, for he knows what is coming. 'Isn't it about time you were finished with that file?' I will sink back in my chair. And Eric will offer up some vague excuse about the fragmentariness of the evidence, the difficulty of establishing connexions – all of which I will cut short by saying, with a faint sigh, 'All right – leave it with me.' And it's then that I will see, beneath his confusion, a look of aggression enter Eric's face; and it's then, as he betrays himself by a momentary glance round my office, that I shall see the substance of that aggression. Envy; envy and hate. For I was once a junior like Eric; he and I were virtual equals. We stood each other drinks at lunch-time and swopped each other's jokes. And now I sit behind a big desk, with a salary to match, promoted by an extraordinary stroke of luck (or, some say, secret machination) to a senior rank in my early thirties; and why shouldn't Eric, who is no different from me, and only a year younger, have and deserve these things too?

I stand by the partition with this scene already scripted and rehearsed, as it were, ahead of me. But it is not really Eric I am looking at. And all that I've said so far about how I treat Eric – how do you know that I haven't made it up, it's not all in my imagination? It's not really Eric I'm looking at. For, after all, Eric sits in my place, just as I sit in Quinn's, and what I see are only the reproduced symptoms of a year ago. It is my life I see through the partition. My life. For this new role that has been mine for six months is not my life. I go through its motions, I wear its mask, but inside is a man just like Eric. And I like to think that it was just the same for Quinn as he stood in this same spot looking at me. Perhaps that is why he had the partition built – in order to see better, to get a clearer view.

So how little Eric knows what I am really looking at as he bends over his work. And how little he knows if he thinks in his bewilderment, beset by all those misleading files, those gaps in the shelves – for perhaps, after all, I was not making it up – by my ever increasing strangeness (has Prentis really gone loopy like his Dad?), that the confusions cease, the mysteries stop, when promotion lifts you up into the rarefied air.

The mysteries don't stop . . .

Marian and the kids look at me each night when I return home, with the thankful expression of people who no longer have to doubt or disbelieve what they see. Perhaps my transformation is a mystery to them, too. Or perhaps their explanation – the explanation which relaxes the looks in their faces – is simple. All Daddy needed was a little power. When he didn't have it, he tried to make up for it by acting the tyrant with us. But now that he has it, we go free. Contentment is just a fortuitous apportioning of power. And they don't ask – any more than they did before – what I do in the office. And that is just as well. For I don't tell them, either. They don't ask if I am tormenting some poor underling in their stead. Why should they, if that is the price of their comfort?

But I don't believe this explanation alone will ever satisfy Marian, for whom I am not so much a transformed as a reformed man: the man I was, years ago, before Mum's death and Dad's breakdown, before the kids grew up. I don't believe she thinks it is power. And perhaps she even has some inkling – sometimes I feel it on those evenings when I work particularly late – of what I'm really doing at the office; that what I am doing is not just what I'm required to do. And what I'm doing isn't just another, idiosyncratic version of power, whatever Quinn may have said – for he could afford the luxury of a little self-reproach, the rescue-launch of retirement standing by. It is only the sort of furtive, underhand and not even original daring of a man who isn't really powerful or daring at all. The sort of daring that knows sooner or later – does Marian know this too? – it will be found out. For one day Eric may say: 'Look, perhaps I shouldn't say this, but . . .'

And I don't believe that Martin is satisfied by the power theory either. For when he looks at me, though I am a more sufferable father than I was, there is still the same disrespect, the same edge of contempt, the same undeluded penetration in his eyes. He doesn't see a man with power; he sees the same old weakling. The only difference is that I no longer conceal it. And this brings into Martin's eyes – even into Martin's eyes – the slightest hint of perplexity. For this is something he cannot understand. But I don't attempt to enlighten him, or to iron out the differences which exist between us, which seem to me less and less a matter of attitude than of simple physiology.

About a fortnight or so after the official notice of my promotion I had the television reinstated in the living room. Call it an act of atonement towards my family. I didn't want it back myself. I feared, for the sake of a gesture, a return to those days of non-communication with my sons and the spectacle of their young minds sopping up trivia. But this didn't happen. The Bionic Man was still running, leaping, focusing his telescopic eyes on distant targets, overcoming all kinds of insuperable difficulties with effortless ease, just as he must have been, unwatched by us, all through the summer – and as he must do, for ever, electronically proofed against mortality. But I noticed Martin was no longer watching his hero's antics with total enthralment. More than once, instead of gasping, he laughed – not a sympathetic laugh but a scoffing laugh, the sort of laugh which, if you interpret it carefully, means: I don't need the tricks of this synthetic hero, I have my own hero – *me*.

And then one day – miracle of miracles – Martin was not watching the Bionic Man. He was out on the common – and not spying on his father coming home from the station, either. He was simply out there to mooch about, the way kids do when they reach a certain age, to look for what might turn up, and to advertise his ever more assertive presence. Now that he has moved to secondary school, an upheaval which hasn't perturbed him in the least, he has gone in for this cult of self-promotion in a big way. He is constantly pushing himself to the fore (so Marian tells me, who seems to have a secret intuition for such things) amongst his fellow pupils; he has actually taken earnestly to the sports field; he is caught admiring himself in the bathroom mirror. In fact, he is undergoing – and coping blithely with – all those changes which normally occur to a boy two or three years older than himself.

And so when I think of Martin as he will be in only a

few years' – who knows, only a year's – time, I think of a creature almost wholly alien to me and therefore beyond contention or ill-feeling. I see him as one of those cocksure, invincible, infallible youths, who will not have to swot to be bright at school, for whom puberty will be a doddle, for whom life will hold no traps, no fears.

But Peter – Peter who is still addicted to the Bionic Man – is another story.

No, if they think it is power, they are wrong. It is not power at all.

And if their new-found contentment somehow depends on their ignorance of what I am really up to in my job – doesn't that prove the main point? Doesn't that encourage me along the path Quinn opened up to me? All these little bits of poisoned paper I am slowly dropping into oblivion. What people don't know, can't hurt them . . .

I still go to see Dad on Wednesdays and Sundays. He still sits on the wooden bench, gazing before him, as indestructible, in his silent impenetrability, as the Bionic Man himself. I have not yet put to him those fatal questions which at one and the same time might restore and destroy my father. Did you betray your fellow-agents? Did you really escape from the Château? Did you sleep with Z's wife? In my mind these questions sound like the key-notes of some fresh interrogation, and Dad has already undergone one interrogation, already endured trials enough. And why should his own son appear to him in the role of interrogator – as the ghost of fat-cheeks, grey-hair and '*le goret*', all rolled into one? Sometimes I see how easily this red-brick mental hospital, with its tranquil gardens, could turn, in the instant, from a place of refuge to a place of torture. And when I ask myself what my motive might be in putting those questions, I find myself wondering whether it would really be to see at last, after the restorative shock, a flash of recognition cross those eyes; or whether it would be to exult over the confession of some ignoble truth. And it seems to me that I care very little for the morals, the rights and wrongs of the case – whether Dad betrayed those three agents, whether he slept with another man's wife. My feelings would not be immensely changed towards a father guilty of those acts. But what does interest me, intensely, exclusively – is whether Dad cracked. For, as with Martin, you see, it is perhaps a matter not of attitude but of physiology.

But I know I won't ever ask those fatal questions. And I won't make further inquiries of my own. All this was decided that evening at Quinn's. Perhaps that means that Dad will never return from the land of silence. But then I sometimes think, with the knowledge I have but don't show Dad, and the knowledge Dad perhaps has and be-lieves I don't, our relations could not be more finely tuned than they are. Every time we sit on that wooden bench, which has often seemed to me like some uneasily rocking see-saw, there are no longer those sensations of tilting and swaying – as if by some mutual, tacit arrangement, we have found the perfect balance.

And if the way I am talking suggests that, behind all my reticence, I really do believe that Dad did all those things that X accused him of, and that, indeed, is the reason for my reticence, then let me assure you that that question, too, hangs like a finely poised balance. For a long time I would still read *Shuttlecock*; I still pored over its pages, though I was no more certain of what I hoped to find there. And often I found myself asking: the smell of apple logs? the sentry urinating against the Château wall? the woman at Frécourt (in whom – was this my imagination? – there was some faint reflection of my mother)? – all these are too particular, too vivid and intimate to be inventions. And, again: would a man narrating a *fictitious* escape be at such pains to describe how he was naked?

And then one day (if you want to know, it was only last month, when suddenly buds were on the trees again and I remembered it was a year since Quinn first dropped that hint about my promotion) I stopped reading Dad's book. I inquired no further. How much of a book is in the words and how much is behind or in between the lines? Perhaps it is best not to probe too deeply into those invisible regions, but to accept on trust what is there on the page as the best showing the author could make. And the same is true perhaps of *this* book (for it has grown into a book) which I have resumed now after a six months' lapse, only to bring to its conclusion. Once you have read it, it may be better not to peer too hard beneath the surface of what it says – or (who knows if you may not be one of those happily left in peace of mind by my 'work' at the department?) what it doesn't say.

34

'Marian,' I say (she is still talking to her plants), 'do you believe in the pathetic fallacy? That it's really a fallacy, I mean?'

35

And today – a Sunday – I forwent for the first time one of my visits to Dad. I said to Marian and the kids yesterday evening (for I knew it was going to be one of those hot, cloudless, high-summer Sundays that sometimes come even in early May): 'Let's go out for the day tomorrow. Let's go to Camber Sands.' And Marian looked at me, as much as to say: 'But aren't you going to see Dad?' And the kids, as much as to say, 'What about Grandpa Loony?' But they did not say these things, and their expressions of surprise soon melted. They are a shrewd family.

Why Camber Sands? There are other parts of the coast which are shorter and easier drives from our part of London. Sentimental reasons. It was here that Marian and I used to come when Martin was scarcely beyond the crawling stage; and not just because in the soft sands of the dunes a small baby could come to very little harm, but because in the hollows of those same dunes it was possible for a young couple, with a little circumspection, to spread a blanket and make warm, airy outdoor love.

But it was here too – and it was only because of this that I was to return later with Marian – that I used to be

taken as a boy, when we stayed for weekends with Uncle
Nigel, a colleague of Dad's in the engineering business,
who had a country cottage near Rye. And what attracted
me then about Camber was less its whispering billows of
sand and wheeling black-headed gulls (for this was before
Mr Forster and his Nature Study classes) but the relics
of the war that still littered the region. Rusting tangles of
metal to waylay landing-craft; huge, zig-zagging rows of
concrete teeth waiting to snap at German tanks; pill-boxes
marking the dykes on Romney Marsh. All this was scenery
from that awesome drama in which Dad had only recently
been an actor (these were the late forties and early fifties).
And looking out at the grey, flat English Channel, which
in that part of the coast retreats to a sullen distance at low
tide, I would have a vision of the war as a simple, romantic
affair of opposing powers. I would think of watchers on
the shore with telescopes; of the dim line of the horizon
hiding on its further side massing, unknown forces. I
dabbled amongst the rusty iron. Perhaps as I did so – who
knows? – Mum and Dad made love, circumspectly, in the
dunes. The tide would come in, slick, shallow and frothy
– and the incoming tide, as every child knows, is an enemy
invader.

And now, invaded and littered in another way – by
caravan-sites and chalets, beach-side cafés and amusement
arcades – Camber Sands still retains these old savours of
love and war. Don't ask me why, knowing that this spot
must be even more spoilt, even more strewn with seaside
junk since Marian and I last saw it, I should still determine
on going there – I who have this hankering for untouched
countryside and have often harangued and bored my
family with conservationist lectures. Perhaps certain things

are inside us and we don't have to go searching for the appropriate setting in order to find them. Or if they aren't inside us, then – perhaps we should admit it – they aren't anywhere.

We packed a picnic bag, blankets, towels, swimming things, sun-tan oil, and set off early. I slipped into our car boot my cricket bat and a ball (for there is no finer cricket ground than the damp flat sands of Camber when the tide is out). But I would not push the point. Peter sat in the back seat with Marian. He was excited. In the rear-view mirror I saw his wide eyes keep darting to things outside the window, the way children's eyes do when they are being taken to the seaside – as if they are crossing a continent. Martin sat in the front beside me, silent and aloof. He was eleven years old and was already affecting to be above such things as family trips to the sea.

Sure enough, Camber, even so early in the season, had fallen prey to the paraphernalia demanded by the holiday-maker and the tripper. Martin cocked up his head at this. He would gladly, perhaps, have spent all day in the cafés and amusement arcades, learning the arts of the seaside hustler. But we tramped a long way from our parked car, till we found a relatively secluded hollow among the dunes; and even on young go-getters in the making, the sun and the sea exert their pull. In a few minutes Martin, no less than Peter, had slipped into bathing trunks; and they were off, down the slopes of the dunes, running across the corrugated sands to confront that great brooding invader.

I watched them. The tide was out at its furthest point, so they had no small distance to cover. By the time they reached the water they would be just two more of several indistinguishable, limbed dots moving in the silvery margins where sea met land. Martin was already several yards ahead of his brother and clearly set on making no allowances for Peter's shorter pace. He was bent on getting this primal seaside ritual over with as soon as possible, on accomplishing it with the maximum of athletic ease and the minimum of childish fuss. His stride was rhythmic and arrogant. Peter's was still the furious, labouring dash of an infant, in which was plainly visible his despair of keeping up with his brother. Half way between the dunes and the sea their bodies lost tone; I could no longer discern Peter's maroon, Martin's blue trunks, and they were distinguishable only by their stature and gait. Two naked, fleeing creatures. And suddenly they were no longer running towards the sea, but running, being impelled, towards the future – another sea of sorts – and their bodies travelling over the sand were mapping the course of things to come. Martin, with never a look back. Peter, doomed always to chase that flying image of his brother, who would run better than him, swim better and, in all things, act more surely than him; doomed to pant after it but never to catch it up. Peter, who will feel in later years, much more than his brother ever will, the odd stab of nostalgia for the salt air and the dunes of Camber Sands; who already possesses the harassed, irresolute looks of his father, and who already has – for I saw it for the first time, as he struggled up again, over the lip of the dunes, a full minute after his brother, breathless and tense, a thread of seaweed stuck to his leg – the hard knot which his father has between the brows, which bespeaks a kind of cruelty.

Peter: 'What are those rusty metal things over there, Dad?'

Dad: 'Oh, they're something left over from the war.'

(As Dad and Peter – Martin having slunk off, to the beach cafés perhaps, or to disturb loving couples in the dunes – walk out again – walk and not run – to the water's edge, which has now drawn considerably nearer; and Dad thinks, almost for the first time, that day, of his own Dad.)

Peter: 'Oh.' (Unenlightened, unwilling to display ignorance by asking further questions, but just a little bit afraid, gripping his father's hand, that the rusty metal things might still be dangerous. And all this suddenly and literally washed away by Dad's visible recoil and audible gasp of cowardice at the icy temperature of the water which has just licked over his foot.)

But this was later. After lunch, after trips for ice-creams, after a deadly earnest cricket match in which Martin suddenly revealed himself for a murderous fast bowler, and after – even while that first trip to the water's edge, that first trip to the future and back, was taking place – Marian and I made love in the sand. We had to be quick, quick as sparrows – you never know when someone might appear over the crest of the dunes. Need for haste; but none for hinting or persuasion, nor for pointless sophistication. All those laborious bedroom antics, to return at last to burrowing in the sand. The beach-grass waved; the gulls floated, white fragments in the blue above. But this would have been Marian's view. My view was filled with sand, a miniature dune-scape, a whole shifting and rippling Sahara that was forming and reforming round our blanket. I thought, it is the landscape of the desert, bleached and smooth-contoured, that most approximates to human flesh. If any landscape can be called naked, it is a landscape of dunes; and perhaps that is the true source of my nostalgia for Camber Sands. And then these same soft-gold hues and gentle contours made me think of the pale, furred creature who was the cause of my beginning these pages, and I remembered the magical words Mr Forster had spoken when I was a boy (Peter's age): 'a piece of nature'.

picador.com

blog
videos
interviews
extracts